# The Lady in Blue

## NOEL BROCK

*A Family's Memoir*

**TRAFFORD**

· Canada · UK · Ireland · USA ·

© Copyright 2005 Noel Brock.
All rights reserved. No part of this publication may be reproduced, stored in a retrieval system, or transmitted, in any form or by any means, electronic, mechanical, photocopying, recording, or otherwise, without the written prior permission of the author.
Contact author at noelbrock@cox.net or www.noelbrock.com

Note for Librarians: A cataloguing record for this book is available from Library and Archives Canada at www.collectionscanada.ca/amicus/index-e.html
ISBN 1-4120-6995-5

Printed in Victoria, BC, Canada. Printed on paper with minimum 30% recycled fibre. Trafford's print shop runs on "green energy" from solar, wind and other environmentally-friendly power sources.

## TRAFFORD PUBLISHING

*Offices in Canada, USA, Ireland and UK*

This book was published *on-demand* in cooperation with Trafford Publishing. On-demand publishing is a unique process and service of making a book available for retail sale to the public taking advantage of on-demand manufacturing and Internet marketing. On-demand publishing includes promotions, retail sales, manufacturing, order fulfilment, accounting and collecting royalties on behalf of the author.

**Book sales for North America and international:**
Trafford Publishing, 6E–2333 Government St.,
Victoria, BC v8t 4p4 CANADA
phone 250 383 6864 (toll-free 1 888 232 4444)
fax 250 383 6804; email to orders@trafford.com

**Book sales in Europe:**
Trafford Publishing (UK) Limited, 9 Park End Street, 2nd Floor
Oxford, UK ox1 1hh UNITED KINGDOM
phone 44 (0)1865 722 113 (local rate 0845 230 9601)
facsimile 44 (0)1865 722 868; info.uk@trafford.com

**Order online at:**
trafford.com/05-1906

10 9 8 7 6 5

Although the story of Alice is true,
the names have been changed
to protect the haunted.

Warmest regards,
Noel Brock

Dedicated to
Callun

In loving memory of
Cokey

"*The Lady in Blue* is about a family. They just happen to have a family ghost. This charming memoir looks back on American life a century ago. The continuity through generations to the present creates a feeling of belonging. This glimpse into their strong loving bonds conjures nostalgic memories of old movies and a family the way we all want ours to be. Warm and inviting, this recollection is a personal journey of everyday events as well as whimsical mysterious happenings. While the ghost is an elusive part of their lives, she is also the thread that binds them, decade after decade, home to home. *The Lady in Blue* is a tribute to families. The mystery is compelling, the paranormal events are fascinating; however, the quality that makes this story memorable and palpable is the enduring family relationships. The strength of *The Lady in Blue* is more than its anecdotes on the supernatural. The pervasive tone is peace, not only in this life but in the life after." — Charol Messenger, book editor, author of *Recognizing Your Natural Intuition, Petals of Self-Discovery, I'm Dancing As Fast As I Can.*

"After reading *The Lady in Blue*, I find myself listening late at night … wishing I could hear footsteps."— Reader, Savannah, Georgia

"*The Lady in Blue* … feel the warmth of family nurtured by joy and adversity and capture the essence of a ghost's journey to her destiny. Ms. Brock tells a compelling story that will make you laugh and cry at the same time."— Reader, Tampa, Florida

# ACKNOWLEDGEMENTS

Special thanks to Abby
who encouraged me to write this book.

Jen, Cassie, and Ron
who helped me remember our many encounters with Alice.

Cami, my darling daughter,
who finally has accepted that my house *is* haunted.

My beloved son, Lane,
for putting up with me and Alice and sharing his stories.

My dearest husband, Frank,
for his patience and making many trips with me to Florida.

My editor, Charol Messenger,
for her careful consideration of every word and respecting my voice.

My gratitude to the cover designer, Karen Saunders,
the cover painter, Joshua Been, and
my publishing advisors, Adrianna and Alexandra.

# PREFACE

Enjoying a good ghost story is a favorite American pastime. Experiencing a ghost in person is another matter. Paranormal sightings cause much excitement and haunted-house anecdotes generate great curiosity.

This story I share with you is my family's personal journey with an intriguing family ghost. The death of a young lady one hundred years ago in a coastal Florida town is connected to a haunted house in central Georgia in 2004. Everyone who says it isn't so has not been to my grandparents' house in Florida or my home in Georgia.

As much as I would like to divulge to you the exact locations of these two special dwellings, to provide this information would invade the privacy of the families involved. For this reason, many of the towns mentioned in *The Lady in Blue* have been given fictitious names. All of the events, however, are factual and historically accurate. The characters are very real people but their names also have been changed. If any name seems familiar, it is purely coincidental. Thank you for allowing me to protect the haunted while the Cason and Carr families share our incredible story.

For the readers who love a good ghost story, enjoy! Just remember, the events really happened.

*Human things must be known to be loved,*
*but Divine things must be loved to be known.*
Blaise Pascal

# PROLOGUE

When I was a teenager, I wanted to tell the story of Alice, but I didn't know how. Today, over thirty years later, there is so much more to tell and I feel to have told it earlier would have done a grave injustice to Alice. I can still feel my childish awe of the nighttime bumps in the night and, later, my breathtaking fear of the woman in blue. Alice has been so real to me for parts of my life, connecting and reconnecting as needed. At first, it was for her. Now I have come to realize, it was for me.

The story is set in a lovely—but haunted—old house on the Halifax River on the east coast of Florida. The intriguing tales of the old home place, built in the late 1880s, are probably more credible than the stories that surfaced in later years. Who would believe that a modern brick home in middle Georgia has its very own ghost… and that the two are connected?

As I take you through several family generations—the Carr's on my grandmother Wanda's side; and the Cason's through her marriage to my wonderful grandfather, Denny—please be patient. I myself have only recently realized that Alice has been trying to tell us she was here and why.

In 1937, when my mother and her family moved into the rambling, white-frame home on the riverfront property, the rooms needed enlarging to accommodate the family. While working within one of the wall partitions, a contractor found a yellow-gold and diamond engagement ring with the engraved name *Alice*. One of the workmen immediately noticed the name was also etched on the dining-room windowpane. Later, when the beautiful girl with long brown curls started walking the halls of the home, it was only right to name her Alice.

# BOOK ONE

### *Cassie and Jo*

*Arranging long-locked drawers and shelves*
*Of cabinets, shut for years,*
*What a strange task we've set ourselves!*
*How still the lonely room appears!*
*How strange this mass of ancient treasures,*
*Mementos of past pains and pleasures.*

— Charlotte Bronte

# CHAPTER 1

A soul in distress is yearning.
Listen to hear what she'll say:
*The depth of the tides is turning.*
*If only my love could stay.*

## 1937
## Shady Hill, Florida

The white clapboard house on the Halifax River is a perfect fit for the Cason family. Wanda and Denny have raised their three children in a small two-story home a block back from Riverview Drive. Although only one story, the new home is spacious and faces the water. They will have gentle daytime breezes, gorgeous sunsets, and picturesque moonlit reflections.

Before moving day, a construction crew enlarges the living room by removing a wall between two small rooms, adds an addition of two bedrooms and one bath, and remodels the kitchen. It is in this wall, between the dining room and new bedrooms, that the diamond engagement ring is found, with the name *Alice* and a small heart engraved in a dainty script. Even the workmen comment that the diamond in the ring must have been used to etch the name on the glass of the dining-room windowpane.

Hugh, the oldest of the Cason children, talks to the workmen. "I wonder who this Alice is?"

"Who she *was*, son," says the painter in multi-colored spattered coveralls. He looks around. "Something bad happened to this Alice woman. I guarantee it."

Hugh shrugs.

The slight-of-build painter continues. "There's a story she's trying to tell. Like my Granny Nolan would say, 'Listen. It is not only words you can hear.'"

Hugh doesn't hear anything. Muscular from working with his father at their automotive shop, and tan from long hours at the beach, the seventeen-year-old merely responds, "See ya later, guys."

The construction foreman calls after Hugh. "Give the ring to your mom. She might want to sell it."

Hugh is happy to take the tiny ring to Wanda. He wants to ask his mom something anyway. "Can I have the afternoon off? The attic in the old house is empty, and the boxes are in the garage."

Wanda nods, examining the piece of jewelry and gingerly running her finger over the diamond solitaire set deep in the gold band. Sun rays from the open window catch the brilliance of the diamond. Wanda's black eyes sparkle. "I'll put this ring in a safe place," she says. "I expect there's a story that goes with it."

However, Alice and her story are soon forgotten. Hugh heads back to their old neighborhood where he meets up with Donna

## The Lady in Blue

Sue, Jean, and Ruthie at Wilma's Drug and Soda Fountain Shop. The four are soon on their way to the sandy beach and the perfect waves of the Atlantic. Jean carefully drives her father's new black Ford coupe, avoiding the largest ruts in the shell asphalt. As they bounce along in the rumble seat of Jean's car, Hugh smiles. His jet-black hair blows in the wind and Ruthie notices how perfectly his eyes match the blue sky of the summer day. She's never seen such a contrast to his mother's dark eyes. *He must have his father's eyes*, she thinks.

Finally, moving day comes. Hugh is glad to have his own bedroom, even if it is off the dining room. While Hugh places his clothes in his new closet, Hoagy Carmichael's music is playing on the radio. Hugh isn't very talkative as a rule, but today he exclaims how much he will love living on the river.

Cassie, fifteen, is happy to share her room with her ten-year-old sister, Jo. After all, they shared a room at the old house. Cassie hangs white iliac curtains in their room, and Jo carefully makes their double bed with the pale-yellow bedspread.

Everyone is excited to be in the new riverfront home. Well, everyone except Jo. For once, she is being very quiet. She hates leaving the only house in which she has ever lived.

As the baby of the family, Jo loves hearing the stories of her birth in the old home place. Her mother, Wanda, and Wanda's sister, Aunt Kelly, have always told her how she was a miracle baby to survive her premature birth. They show Jo the drawer of the bedroom dresser that was her first baby bed because she arrived so early that no one was prepared. They tell her how the family physician, Dr. Sawyer, gave up on saving Jo and turned to save Wanda's life. Aunt Kelly always chimes in describing how she grabbed the lifeless tiny bundle from the newspapers on the floor and spanked and shook it until she heard a cry. Aunt Kelly had lost three of her own babies at birth and was determined that Wanda would not lose one of hers. Even Zeb, their old stooped gardener who still works for them, opens his hand and points to his palm where Jo's tiny head fit for months during her early life.

Wanda remembers the many trips with Jo to Duke University Hospital in North Carolina. Surgery had to be performed to correct Jo's poorly developed mastoid bones in her inner ears and to remove her tonsils and adenoids. After four surgeries, the recurring deafness was no longer a problem.

Wanda is just happy that the health problems caused by the premature birth were not more severe. No one could guess now that Jo was born at twenty-six weeks. Her dark curls frame her precious but impish face that belies her years of pain and suffering. Jo loves everyone she meets and they, in turn, love her.

Cassie, although five years older, has a special bond with her younger sister, which probably started because of Jo's delicacy during her early childhood. While Cassie is unpacking their belongings from the old house, she picks up Jo's tap-dance shoes and laughs, remembering the day when she and her six-year-old sister were left in the car while their mother, Wanda, went into Belz Department Store. Then Jo, who was in Cassie's care, jumped out of the car and started tap dancing on the sidewalk of Main Street. When their mother came out of the store, she was horrified to see passersby throwing coins at the sidewalk entertainment. Jo, on the other hand, was proud of her entrepreneur accomplishment. Cassie remembers even now her mother's reproving dark eyes. "Cassie, what is going on here?" Cassie decided it was best not to try to explain.

Cassie's thoughts return to the present and she unloads another box, still laughing. That was not the last time Jo was more than Cassie could handle.

At last, all of the Cason belongings are in their new home. The single-story house is spacious and open. Wanda is glad she doesn't have to climb stairs any more, and she loves the breezes off the riverfront that blow through the porch windows.

Denny is pleased that Wanda has a bigger kitchen. He knows how his wife whirls around making delectable dishes in no time. At least that's how it seems to him. When he comes home from his shop for lunch, the smell of pork chops, okra, tomatoes, and fresh corn or other delicious vegetables, always greets him. Thankfully, the fresh produce market is as close to Riverview Drive as from their old home on Mimosa Lane.

During the summer, with relatives visiting from Georgia, without a doubt warming in the oven will be the best fresh peach cobbler they ever tasted. It never ceases to amaze Denny how Wanda has lunch prepared when some folks are still eating breakfast. Every day, when the children leave for school and Denny goes to work, Wanda drives to Zelda's Produce Shed. The results are shared with the family—and others who happen to come by at mealtime.

Wanda, an immaculate housekeeper, quickly puts the new home in order. She is a conservative spender and looks for a few items the family needs for their roomier but more formally decorated home. Family heirlooms and generous gifts from older friends, such as Mrs. Whitman next door, make the Cason's new Riverview Drive home a special place. It was Mrs. Whitman who told Wanda, at the Riverview Garden Club one day, that the house on the river was for sale.

On one of Wanda's shopping sprees, she buys a new platform rocker, which she places beneath the wide archway between the living room and dining room, and lays a family-heirloom gold-and-white tapestry over the back. The solid-oak rocker is a beautiful and useful addition to the area.

Cassie first notices the rocker that night, right after the family says their goodnights. "Mom, I love the new chair," Cassie says. "It's so perfect for this house."

Cassie didn't know just how perfect. Catching a movement out of the corner of her eye, she jerks around. Something is definitely not right.

She doesn't comprehend at first what she's seeing and stares in disbelief. "Mom, Dad, come quick!"

After the initial shock that overwhelms them all, the Casons hold hands and watch. What meets their eyes amazes them. The platform rocker is rocking… and no one is in it. In the dim light, the tapestry

## The Lady in Blue

is swinging back and forth as the chair rocks. The teenagers are too enthralled to be terrified. Wanda says, "Oh, my! Oh, my!"

The next night, they all hurry to the living room to again observe the chair and they are not disappointed. Only late at night does the chair rock… and rock and rock. For the next ten years or so, when the shades are drawn and the lights are turned low, it rocks.

# CHAPTER 2

*Spirits there must be in this old house,*
*A platform chair back and forth to rock.*
*Misty moonlight beams vaguely yet ominously,*
*And chimes like music from the hallway clock.*

## 1938

After a year in their Riverview Drive home, Cassie and Jo know they live in a haunted house. Their parents' early-to-bed, early-to-rise routine isolates Wanda and Denny from the nocturnal episodes of slamming doors, unscheduled clock chimes, and shadows on the walls. However, the sisters do hear their parents talking in the master bedroom when they think they're alone. Obviously they are aware of the ghost.

*The presence,* as Cassie calls it, is nameless until late one night. Jo is still up studying for exams when she looks up and sees Cassie standing in front of the gold-framed mirror over the dining buffet. Jo doesn't recognize the long, layered, blue-dotted Swiss dress that Cassie is wearing; and her long brown hair is swept up on top of her head.

In the shadows of the elegant crystal chandelier reflecting in the mirror, Jo tries to make eye contact with Cassie, to give her the look that says, *What in the heck are you doing?* Instead of looking into Cassie's eyes, however, in the mirror Jo sees only herself. Cassie has disappeared!

Jo runs into their back bedroom and flings open the door. Cassie is asleep, dressed in pajamas, and her soft brown hair *is* up on her head… in twenty curlers!

Very quickly Jo concludes three things: The spirit inhabiting this house is a young woman. She looks a lot like Cassie. Most important, she has a name. The engagement ring and the windowpane inscription were clues after all. Her name is *Alice*.

# CHAPTER 3

*Many strange things,*
*A slowly opened door,*
*A quiet foot across the wooden floor.*

## 1939

## *The Cason Sisters*

Life could not be better for these two teenage girls growing up at the coast. During the summer, there's a different concert every night at the Boardwalk; Sunday evenings, all of the churches combine services at the Band Shell. Cassie was ten when construction on the south end of the Boardwalk started; the Band Shell was built just last year. Now there are more excuses to be on the beach side of town.

The Fourth of July is celebrated over several days, with beauty contests, amateur wrestling and boxing contests, parades, stock car races, junk car races, and motorcycle races—all on the beach. The stock car races on the long stretch of quartz sand started in 1936; other kinds of races as early as 1903. Always, there are fun things to do with their family and friends. The Fourth this year is more patriotic than the usual fanfare. It's only been twenty-five years since World War I and trouble is brewing again in Europe.

Cassie runs to get a seat at the Band Shell. "Hurry up, Jo!" Meg and Nellie wave for the Cason sisters to join them for the brilliant fireworks in front of the Boardwalk. They all sit just as a burst of yellow, red, orange, and blue illuminates the night sky. As always, the spectacular finale starts after a wonderful day.

Despite Jo's health problems, she leads a very active life: dancing, singing, and expression lessons. Her tap-dance performances are now tastefully done in hotels and dance halls. Jo, who has never met a stranger, loves to be part of any social function.

Cassie is enjoying her senior year of high school. At only five feet tall and ninety pounds, she is the smallest girl in her class. At proms, dances and socials—any excuse for fun—she cannot decide if Glenn Miller or Benny Goodman has the best swing music. And swing dance she does, whenever she gets the chance!

Friends are in and out of their house on Riverview Drive. The young people see the empty rocking chair moving late at night and, at first, are amazed. After that, for many the wonder in their eyes turns to fear. Real friends learn to accept Alice and come again. Della Mayes is the only one who refuses to step foot inside the Cason family house ever again. Jo's opinion is that it's Della's loss, not theirs.

Cassie and Jo can't contain their excitement the day they get their first boat—a rowboat with oars. It's a major undertaking to row across the half-mile stretch to the other side of the Halifax River.

Noel Brock

Oblivious to the deep channel over which their little boat is crossing, they row and row, until one of them announces that "thumbitis" has set in. They cheer when they stand on land again. Everyone congratulates them on their bravery and they laugh. Cassie whispers to Meg, "Brave is going home to sleep at night, never knowing what that night will bring."

This weekend particularly evokes fear because their parents have gone to Georgia for an uncle's funeral. Fortunately, Wanda and Denny were able to travel following the aftermath of one of the seasonal tropical storms that frequents this coastal town. They drove in Denny's car, leaving Wanda's new 1939 Plymouth for the girls to have a way to get around. No sooner than the parents have left the city limits of Shady Hill, Cassie eases Wanda's "pride and joy" out of the driveway and the girls head to town with Jo humming one of her chorus lines. Because of the recent storm damage, only one other car is on the streets. Unfortunately, that black coupe, driven by the maid of a wealthy couple from Atlanta, crashes right into their mama's white sedan.

Horrified, Cassie and Jo get out of their mother's precious car and assess the damage. At the police station, they beg the Atlanta couple to make immediate retribution. With the money paid, the girls go to Charlie, a family friend who is a mechanic, hoping to get the car restored by Monday. However, Charlie needs to order a new door and estimates it will take several weeks to repair the damage and paint the car.

## The Lady in Blue

"Cassie, won't Mom and Dad be home Sunday night?" Jo asks with worry.

Cassie looks as if she might cry. "Yes."

Now the girls' fear of being home alone—with the ghost—is superseded by the fear of their parents returning from Georgia. They call their friend, Meg, who picks them up at Charlie's shop and drives them home. "Have a safe night by yourselves," she tells the sisters and smiles when they groan, knowing the ghost will keep them company.

That night alone in bed, when Cassie hears a door slam, she hollers out, "Jo, is that you?"

Jo appears with her wet hair wrapped in a towel. "No. Whatever it is, I didn't do it. You know Alice is going to be out early tonight. She loves to frighten us when Mom, Dad, and Hugh aren't here."

"Don't go in the living room," Cassie says. "I can't look at that chair tonight." Cassie isn't going anywhere in this house alone. At that moment, the lights go out. "Maybe it's an electrical storm?" Cassie wonders out loud.

Jo looks out one of the windows on the front porch. "No rain. No lightning. No bad weather. The storm has passed."

Cassie wants to stay in bed and forget about their uninvited guest. "This is a slumber party," she announces to no one in particular, "and you are not welcome."

Soft lullaby music fills the air then. Cassie starts to cry, and Jo goes searching for the source of the tune. At the dining room, she

Noel Brock

shivers. The air is icy. Then the tapestry slips off the rocking chair and lands at her feet. "Cassie, help me!"

The sisters hug each other tightly all night long in bed.

# CHAPTER 4

*At first morning light,*
*The ghosts must go*
*To wait for the night*
*In their graves below.*

## 1940
## *Cassie*

Graduation from Beachwood High is a highlight for Cassie. Wearing her white cap and gown, the petite brown-eyed brunette proudly walks up the aisle.

"She is so pretty," Jo comments, thinking about her own future graduation. Jo wants to be a history teacher, although that day seems far away. Right now, she envies Cassie for her new adventures that lie ahead.

The English teachers for the twelfth grade had required the students to give a speech in order to pass the class and graduate. Cassie, being painfully shy, was exempted from the oral speech and permitted to write a report instead. She now smiles *thank you* to Mrs. Burton, the kind English teacher.

Later, Cassie and her friends leave the school to start the round of graduation parties for the night. Happily, Cassie joins the festivities at Leila Holmes' house, a three-story, white-brick mansion on the ocean side of town; in fact, the backyard borders the white sand dunes of the beach. Cassie thinks of her own smaller but very special home and smiles.

Wearing a pale-blue dress with princess lines and a back skirt-panel, Cassie is ready to swing dance. She takes off her shoes and starts moving in rhythm to the tune of "When You Wish Upon a Star." She might be shy but she is a superb dancer.

While dancing, Cassie wonders about Alice, the other young girl who danced on the wooden floors of the Riverview Drive house. Did she know *these* songs? Who hurt Alice to make her so sad?

Last night, while it was storming outside, Cassie heard a noise that sounded like moaning and crying. When she turned over in bed, the darkened windowpane glistened with huge raindrops. The torrents of liquid pooled together and slowly fell, like a giant teardrop.

Over the summer, Cassie ponders Alice and what happened to destroy the young woman's dreams. Both Cassie and Jo experience the late-night appearances, light footsteps, and mournful cries. They sense an indescribable sadness. It's evident that the promised fulfillment of Alice's dreams fell short.

Then Cassie leaves for a small Georgia college to further her own dream of becoming a librarian. Reluctantly, she says goodbye to her family. She really is going to miss Jo and all their fun times. She also thinks of their few scary times and imagines that Jo will probably miss her company, because it is easier to face the ghost with your sister.

Wanda drives her oldest daughter to Dustin, Georgia, and kisses her on the cheek. "Don't forget to write."

With a few of her cousins from Georgia attending the same college, Cassie has great fun. She makes new friends and studies hard and barely has time to think about home. Her cousin, Sonja, reminds her of family and Shady Hill when she tells all their new friends about Alice. Doug, who was just warming up to Cassie, begins to act strangely.

"So much for a new boyfriend," Cassie says to Sonja. "What kind of man lets the tales of a tiny woman in blue bother him?"

No one expected what a void Cassie's absence would create for Jo. She keeps her back to the dining room when she studies at night and, when she's done, holds her breath when she has to cross that room to flip off the light switch.

It's while Cassie is gone that the silver tea service crashes to the floor in the middle of the night—off the middle of the dining-room buffet, all five pieces, including the tray. The hinge on the teapot is broken: proof that the absurdity really happened. Hugh describes to Cassie how a blue light was hovering in his doorway when he first awoke to the sound. For the first time, he starts questioning his bedroom's location—next to the dining room.

Jo wants her sister back home. She misses Cassie driving her around, especially to the beach, and is sorry for all the grief she caused her older sister. Cassie was so shy. Jo always just wanted to have fun. So many of the fun things embarrassed Cassie. Oh, for the good old days when Cassie was home!

Besides, Jo is scared late at night in the house. Last night, she felt Alice brush up against her—as if to hug her—and warm air blew on Jo's neck. The temperature in the room dropped forty degrees. And Cassie wasn't there to talk to about this latest ghostly happening.

It never takes Jo long to recover from her melancholy moments. Tonight is no exception. For the spring dance at Beachwood High, she chooses a long red-satin dress with a V-shaped neckline. The pretty brunette waves goodbye to her parents as she leaves with Penny, her girlfriend. Since the girls are in junior high, they have to meet their "dates" at the school gymnasium. Penny's father drives the two girls to the dance and smiles as they laugh in the backseat.

"Jo, I love your dress," says Penny.

For a moment, Jo is sad again, thinking of her sister. "Thanks. This is Cassie's dress. She let me wear it."

That evening, Wanda hears a loud noise. "Denny, is that Jo coming in from the school party? I hear someone at the back door."

Denny hurries to check. Suddenly he calls out to Wanda who is putting curlers in her hair in the bathroom. "Come quick! Something's wrong with Jo!"

Jo is crumpled in a heap at the back porch. Worried, her parents run out to the stone steps and kneel over their pale daughter. Her red dress is billowing in the wind. She slowly opens her eyes.

"I forgot my keys," she says. "When I couldn't get in the front door, I came around to the back. While I was standing on the steps, someone put their hand on my shoulder. I guess I fainted."

A dutiful father, Denny walks around the yard, checking for a prowler. Slowly he parts the branches of the banana tree, then circles the large orange tree. Jo watches from the porch, grateful that she has a fearless father.

When he returns to the porch, she grabs his arm, recovered from her mishap, and with a long sigh pulls him inside the house. "You know no one is out there." She glances back over her shoulder and locks the door behind them. *For all the good it will do,* she thinks.

# CHAPTER 5

*Oh, say, can you see?*

## 1941
## Denny

The dream of a four-year college education for Cassie comes to an end when the family calls her home after one year. Denny, her father, is sick with typhus fever and their family-owned business is suffering financially without his leadership. Cassie brushes up on her secretarial skills at a business college, then becomes a secretary at the Naval Air Force Auxiliary Station, a branch of Cecil Field located in Jacksonville, Florida. Cecil Field opened in June 1941. Soon after that, construction started on the branch base further south on the coast. President Franklin Delano Roosevelt predicted, "This generation of Americans has a rendezvous with destiny."

While the Auxiliary is still being constructed, Cassie is secretary to the Lieutenant Commander. After the Auxiliary is finished, the United States' involvement in World War II is imminent. The Eu-

## The Lady in Blue

ropean War started on September 1, 1939, when Germany invaded Poland without warning. It was inevitable that the U.S. would join the major world powers in this resistance to the threat of totalitarianism against world peace.

Denny is critically ill with typhus, so sick that even when a major hurricane threatens the eastern Florida coast the Casons cannot leave home. Delusional with fever, he doesn't even realize the waves are crashing against the house or that the boards on the windows are rattling in the gusts and water.

During the hurricane, the family huddles in prayer for Denny and for them all. The crash of breaking glass permeates the air, and the wind howls through the vacant houses on both sides of them; the Whitmans and Cones evacuated yesterday. In the horror of these several days, Cassie does notice one strange thing: the platform rocker is not rocking at night.

Then the winds die, the water subsides, and the house on Riverview Drive is still standing. Denny is still alive and the family physician pays a frantic visit. Dr. Sawyer thinks Denny is better. That night the platform rocker starts rocking again.

# CHAPTER 6

*No airman can believe*
*Bonny lady in a chair.*
*Do these eyes deceive?*
*Now she is not there.*

## 1941
## *The War*

The nation is at war. Shortly before eight a.m. on the morning of December 7, 1941, the Japanese attack the naval base at Pearl Harbor. The Casons are sitting in front of their Majestic tabletop radio, astonished by reports of fighters and dive-bombers emblazoned with the emblem of the Rising Sun who have destroyed seven of the eight battleships at anchor, killing 2,330 Americans and wounding 1,145. The family cries.

The next day, President Roosevelt gives his "Day of Infamy" speech and asks Congress to declare war on Japan. Three days later, the Axis partners—Japan, Germany, and Italy—declare war on the United States, and Congress reciprocates. *Amos and Andy* and *The Lone Ranger* won't be on the radio airwaves for a long while.

Living along the Florida coast, the Cason family has a greater

## The Lady in Blue

awareness of the war than folks inland. Denny patrols the beach, watching for submarines. Jo, at fifteen, is an airplane spotter. Cassie works at the Naval Air Station as secretary to the Chief Clerk in the Administration Building. Wanda feeds the family the best she can; but food is scarce, especially meat. Gas is rationed, as are other commodities.

When it's announced that there will be a shortage of tires, Denny buys four extra tires and puts them in the attic—only to bring them down a few days later when the military sends out a plea. Roosevelt calls on the United States to be the "great arsenal of democracy" and to help supply the Allies with materials needed. To the Casons, the donation of the tires is a minor contribution, because they already have made the greatest possible sacrifice: sending their only son and brother, Hugh, into the Army.

Driving over the bridge to the ocean side of the city requires special identification passes; any car on the road at night has to navigate without lights. To protect the shoreline from raids and submarine attacks, every home must have heavy shades to block out all light. The Cason home becomes a favorite hangout for airmen from the Auxiliary. Behind drawn shades, as midnight approaches, they watch the rocking chair methodically swinging back and forth. By now, the airmen know about Alice and call her by name. That the rocker is empty is forgotten. It is now "Alice's rocker." A few of the guys can even describe her. Yes, she looks a lot like Cassie, with long, dark hair and brown eyes. The pretty lady moves about. Everything about her is small, tiny features, tiny feet.

With the impending battles ahead, Alice brings comfort to the airmen, not the fear one would expect.

"Neissler, you see that?"

"Yeah, Kingsley. She's on the prowl tonight."

"Too bad I can't ask her out."

"Go ahead. When you bore her too badly, she'll just disappear."

The two airmen laugh as they leave the Cason home and head back to the base.

"It's wartime, man. A little ghost isn't going to scare me."

Cassie moves to the Central Office to be secretary for the Captain. One of her duties is writing the "killed in action" letters to families of the naval airmen who died in the line of duty. When she starts recognizing friends from high school, the assignment becomes way too personal and the Executive Officer writes the letters himself.

Jo works for a local photographer. Many of the airmen come in to get their pictures made for their military personnel records and love talking to Jo about base gossip. Naturally, Cassie also hears bits and pieces of Auxiliary talk. So, together Jo and Cassie write a gossip column for the base newspaper, *The Phantom*. They call their column "Bad Boys' Banter." Everyone loves the weekly scoop, and the sisters love writing the latest news—until Cassie gets a call from the Captain one day. The last column they wrote about Daphnene Linder and Joe Mathews as the newest hottest couple was a big mistake. Daphnene Linder is the wife of a high-ranking official who was not amused to see his wife's flagrant indiscretions with

## The Lady in Blue

the handsome young recruit discussed in the base gossip column. Because Jo and Cassie didn't know Daphnene was not a single lady, they are forgiven; however, the snafu ends their journalistic days. The airmen cannot understand why the Cason sisters did not feature Alice in their gossip column. "Now that would be a story to tell!" And a lot safer to write about.

One night, a PBY patrol plane needing repair lands on the Halifax River in front of the Cason house. Early the next morning, Jo and Cassie row over in their little boat to investigate. A naval rescue boat has arrived to assist the disabled plane. When the plane is ready to take off, the sisters have to board the twenty-two-foot crash boat so the waves won't wash them overboard. One of the airmen temporarily ties the girls' row boat to the larger boat. He recognizes the girls and instantly inquires about Alice. For any discomfort Alice may bring to the Casons, her ability to distract from the horrors of the war is a welcomed interlude.

One airman, Jake, who visits the family, teases Wanda about their ghostly visitor. Her attitude is if one doesn't say it and doesn't think it, it just isn't so. "Who is this lady in blue you guys keep coming up here to look at?" she asks. "Do I know her?" Wanda doesn't like thinking about Alice or the possible ramifications of more frequent sightings.

Jake puts his arm around Wanda. Even the young guys consider Cassie and Jo's mom a beauty at forty-three. Having protected herself from the summer sun, her porcelain complexion is flawless and her long legs belie her average height.

Noel Brock

Wanda remembers another time when Jake put his arms around her shoulder. Cassie and Jo had gone to town with her but shopped separately from her. When the girls finished their own purchases, they jumped in Wanda's new "Baby," a 1941 two-toned blue Plymouth coupe. Cassie drove and started singing, and Jo spotted two boys. Soon the guys were in the car with the girls and off the four went, up Main Street to near the yacht club and fisherman's wharf. Two hours later, the girls, with Jake and Luke still with them, returned home where Wanda arrived shortly later by bus. "Girls, did you leave something in town—like your mom?"

"Oh, Mom!" Cassie exclaimed as the realization of what they had done hit her.

The girls were really sorry, but Wanda was furious. Jake spoke up, trying to get Wanda in a better humor. "Now, Momma, don't be mad. We're sorry we left you in town." He gave her a winning smile.

"Don't you mama me," she reprimanded.

Now Wanda's thoughts return to the present and she retorts to Jake, "Yeah, Cassie and Jo pick you boys up and you are all riding around in Baby when I come out and find my car gone. Imagine. Your own daughters forgetting they have their mother in town with them."

"But the afternoon was gorgeous," Jake says. "The girls looked spectacular, and Baby was ready to ride." Jake squeezes Wanda's arm. "And you looked so cute getting off the bus in your driveway."

Wanda shakes her soft dark curls and tries to be stern but ends up laughing. Laughter is hard to come by these days with young men going off to war. *The love of fellow countrymen,* Wanda thinks.

The Casons don't like to think of the battles being fought on foreign soils, but as a coastal family, war is a way of life. They believe in the cause of freedom. They see the pain of sacrifice but also see the joy of unification.

Jo is especially loyal. She is so patriotic that when the family is riding in the car and the "Star Spangled Banner" comes on the radio, she makes the driver stop and everyone get out and stand at attention. Once when Wanda stepped out of Baby for the anthem, old Mr. Cramer turned his head to look at her and ran his Ford into a palm tree. For years, Jo thought Mr. Cramer was just excited about the national anthem.

Jo is also loyal to Alice. When her mother, Wanda, talks about replacing the platform rocker with a regular recliner, Jo adamantly refuses to hear of such a thing. Cassie, on the other hand, would like a reprieve from the nighttime visits. It is tiresome to have a ghost.

# CHAPTER 7

*When I come to journey's end,*
*All my love to you I send.*

## Carey

The afternoon of December 5, 1945, five Grumman Avengers take off from Fort Lauderdale's Naval Air Station for a navigational training flight… and all five fail to appear at the specified area. The torpedo planes and fourteen crewmen are never heard from again. The Avengers had carried three-men crews. One lucky airman was late and missed his flight. There is no voice contact, no Mayday call for help. They just disappear. Fourteen airmen gone. No oil slick. No debri. Their loss is assumed to have been caused by the war-time enemy.

A mourning father remembers his airman son. Printed copies of words too painful to speak are found around the Auxiliary:

*Yes, he wanted to fly,*
*To plumb the unknown sea,*
*To make the heavens safe*

# The Lady in Blue

*For earthlings—you and me.*
*Now he sails the sky about us,*
*To his Lord he clings.*
*God has taken the engine*
*And left him only the wings.*

Cassie cannot bear to hear about this latest Bermuda Triangle incident. Tearfully, she relives her own personal tragedy the year before.

It's November 1944 and she is seriously dating a young pilot, Carey, who is in training for the next phase of the war. Pilots of SBD and SNJ planes are sent to either the Great Lakes for carrier training or Vero Beach, Florida, for night-flight training. Carey has been sent to Vero Beach.

One night he switches assignments so another airman can go out with his girlfriend. Seven F-6F Hellcats take off from Vero Beach at dark and are to rendezvous at a certain time. Five of the aircraft fail to appear and cannot be reached by radio. The mission is over the Bermuda Triangle. They are no more.

Before Carey left on his ill-fated mission, he was writing a letter to Cassie. The letter is later sent to his grieving sweetheart. When she arrives home from visiting relatives in Georgia and has no letters from him, she fears the worst.

Noel Brock

    Carey's friend, Paul, has written to Cassie the devastating news, enclosing Carey's incomplete letter and a necklace Carey had just bought for her.

    Cassie's grief is unbearable. A piece of her heart is lost forever in the deep ocean. *Why?* she wonders. Why did she lose the love of her life just three months after she found him? She reads again and again his last words to her, which brings some comfort.

> *All else is doubt, but this will not forsake me:*
> *Here under this or any other sun*
> *Wherever life, wherever death may take me,*
> *You are the one—you are the only one.*

    Cassie cries on her bed, then senses a presence watching her. A cold blast of air moves through the room and she sits up and pulls the covers around her. Then the small, white chair in her bedroom begins rocking. *This rocker never moved before on its own.* Suddenly a calm comes over Cassie and she knows Carey is at peace. She feels his love surround her, and she is no longer afraid.

> *Dear God, tonight we learned the truth.*
> *You have a boy up there who's now in heaven.*
> *He's wearing pilot's wings that shine like new.*
> *So lately were they given.*

# CHAPTER 8

*Just you and me,*
*And ghost makes three.*

## 1945
## *Ron*

Cassie and Ron meet at a Methodist Youth Fellowship meeting. He's been fixed up for a blind date with Jo. However, he sees Cassie and is instantly won over. "I know Jo is in the brown fur coat, but who is the doll in the silver fox coat?"

Actually, Ron recognizes Cassie. He saw her the first day he checked in at Cecil Field and admired her Veronica Lake hairdo, petite frame, gorgeous legs, and prissy walk. Her waist was so tiny that he knew he could get a single hand around it. She was wearing a chic Lauren Bacall street dress with contrasting pockets. His eyes followed her. "I'm going to marry that girl," he remarked out loud.

Ron cannot believe his good fortune. All he has to do is convince Cassie he is the man for her. At a church social that evening, he finds himself "the guesser" of all the girls' waists. The money raised will benefit the Auxiliary. The band plays "Yankee Doodle Boy" and all the girls get in line. When Jo and Cassie walk up, Ron guesses Cassie's waist as one inch smaller than Jo's, although the reverse is true. When he says "nineteen inches," he gets a smile from her and his heart skips a beat.

Cassie isn't sure about this third-class petty officer who arrived in charge of a naval air-force group soon to be sent overseas. They came from Jacksonville where training on SBDs—two-seater dive-bombers—was intense. Each plane has a pilot and a gunner.

Ron still doesn't know the reality of war, although he's starting to get a pretty good idea. He graduated from North Georgia Military College just as the war started, joined the Army and was sent to Georgia Technical Institute. There he saw a notice posted that an exam would be given to find the fifty most qualified men for a special mission for the naval air force. He took the exam and was one of the fifty transferred to this specialized branch of the service.

Cassie is dating the Personnel Officer at the Auxiliary when Ron enters the picture. Dubious, she compares him to her boyfriend, Stan, who is a girl's dream with his sandy hair, blue eyes, and gorgeous tan. However, Ron, with his jet-black hair, green eyes, and winsome smile tugs at Cassie's heart.

Besides being from Georgia, Ron can't dance and he doesn't do the beach scene well. Cassie is horrified when he shows up at the beach in shoes and socks. "How do you stand this sand between your toes?" he asks.

*We are way too different,* she thinks.

## The Lady in Blue

However, Ron is a handsome airman stationed here to fight for his country, so Cassie wants to give him a chance. Besides, he has such an outgoing personality, which compliments her own shy nature.

Then Ron has the audacity to laugh about Alice. *Just wait*, Cassie thinks humorously.

When Ron is shipped out ahead of schedule, sent to San Luis Obispo, California, he believes the old boyfriend, Stan, the Personnel Officer, is responsible. At the California Polytechnical Institute for three months, the reality of war comes closer for Ron and his crew. They are sent to the Western Pacific Ocean, first stop Guam. U.S. troops have been on the island since July 1944 and welcome the reinforcement.

In a letter to Cassie, Ron encloses a bracelet handmade from tiny seashells from another Western Pacific island.

*I am now on Peleliu, writing from the top of a sixty-foot tower where I spend many nights waiting for the dreaded enemy to attack. The Japanese were here first. When the Marines came in, the Japanese retreated to the coral rock caves. They fight on. I am bringing you a Japanese bayonet I brought out of one of the caves—but not the horrific story that goes with it. I would like to think my pretty little brown-haired girl will be waiting for me when and if I return from this war. I thought you and Jo would each like one of these bracelets I made for you.*
*All my love, Ron.*

## Noel Brock

*Can't say where I'm going.*
*Don't know where I'll land.*
*All Airforce maneuvers*
*Must secret remain.*
*Can't say for sure, sweet,*
*These words that I write*
*Will be passed by the censor,*
*So I'll just say goodnight.*

Cassie laughs. The package with Jo's bracelet arrived days before her own. Not quite the impression Ron was trying to make. The waiting part is hard for Cassie because she is falling in love.

Then she sees the postscript, *"How's Alice?"* Wearing the row of miniature conch shells on her wrist, Cassie smiles and walks into the riverfront house that she has called home for eight years.

# CHAPTER 9

*My love, I saw thee once*
*By the light of the moon,*
*In rhythm with the wedding dance.*
*The rest is left to chance.*

## 1946

During some major changes at the Riverview Drive house, Wanda replaces the platform rocker with a gold-and-white fabric recliner, just in time for the wedding. Cassie did wait for Ron and they are moving to Georgia.

Coming home from a movie one afternoon, Jo ponders that this might be the last time she and her sister will go out together. In front of the mirror, Jo admires her red-cropped rayon sailor shirt and shorts, which reminds Cassie of Olivia de Havilland in the movie, *The Best Years of Our Lives*.

"The best years may have been," Cassie says to Jo, "but better ones are ahead."

However, Jo is losing her sister and is also concerned about what Alice will do without her special chair and special friend, Cassie.

"Cassie," Jo says, "do you think Alice will come to the wedding? Wouldn't Ron's mom, Ella, and his Aunt Hilda absolutely swoon?"

Jo remembers last year's visit from the two prim and proper ladies from Georgia when Ella and her sister-in-law visited Ron in Jacksonville during his furlough. Inquisitive by nature, the two women had stopped by Shady Hill to meet their boy's obvious choice for the upcoming engagement. Cassie, being too shy to meet the guests alone, took Jo with her to the bus station. During the brief stopover, the future daughter-in-law met her future mother-in-law. Cassie wore a jade-green floral-print dress with rouched bodice and sleeves. Her three-inch heels made her tiny frame seem even smaller. The petite girl with long, brown hair and dark eyes made a striking picture, but she was so nervous that her appearance was not foremost in her mind.

She need not have worried. Jo kept everyone laughing with anecdotal stories—staying away from war stories, however, such talk being too painful for a mother with two young boys fighting the dreaded Germans and Japanese. Ron's younger brother, George, joined the Navy at age seventeen.

*No Alice tales either,* Jo thought. These ladies were way too straight-laced to accept Alice just yet.

When Ella and Hilda's bus departure was called, they hugged Cassie goodbye until the time they would come back and stay a while. "Come anytime," Jo cut in with a chuckle. "We have a hoot at our house."

## The Lady in Blue

Cassie gave Jo a reproving look, which caused her younger sister to laugh even harder as the bus pulled away.

Wanda and Denny wish Cassie would wait until the war is over before marrying, but they want her to be happy. "I love your engagement ring," her mother tells her, admiring the platinum-and-diamond solitaire, which reminds Wanda of the other ring, the one in her jewelry box for nine years.

Now late summer, as Cassie's wedding preparations begin in earnest, she is disappointed that the special necklace worn by brides on her mother's side of the family can't be found. The filigree lavaliere, kept in the dining-room china cabinet, disappeared last year just before her cousin's wedding. Wanda kept thinking it would show up, but it never did. Other keepsakes related to weddings have also gone missing.

*Obviously, Alice does not like weddings,* Cassie thinks. *What does Alice like? Who is Alice? What does she want from us?*

One afternoon Jo goes to town on a mission to find answers to these questions that she and Cassie have had about Alice. Jo's research at the local library of historical archives reveals that a former occupant of the house—named Alice—died at age nineteen during her engagement to Larry. Based on the details of their research, Jo and Cassie envision what happened that night long ago.

The year is 1905 and the plan is for an autumn wedding. On the coast, the month of October will be perfect because of its pleasant evenings.

Alice is marrying her high-school sweetheart. Her satin-and-lace gown, the bodice outlined with tiny pearls, is being hand-sewn. There is so much to do before October. That is precisely why Alice is at the street party downtown on this hot August night.

It seems like everyone in Shady Hill is at the yacht club. She is listening to a band, the one she wants for her wedding reception. Her aunt is with her. They both move closer to hear the Buddy Bolden Band better and everyone glances at the pretty young girl. She is a dark-haired beauty who takes one's breath away, especially when a dimpled smile crosses her face. She sways to the music and her eyes say, Oh, what fun this is!

Suddenly Alice sees Larry, her fiancé. Excitedly she starts toward him—until she sees her beloved embracing a tall, slender brunette. He leads the exotic-looking woman out onto the dance floor and the song "Careless Love" fills the air. Alice runs tearfully back through the crowd, telling her aunt she wants to go home.

Home is the white-frame house on the Halifax River where she and Larry had their first kiss on the front porch. Moonlit memories flood Alice as she runs. In her bedroom, she flings the engagement ring to the floor where it hits with a thud.

## The Lady in Blue

Later that evening, Larry comes by to visit Alice and finds her in tears at the boat dock. He touches her arm and asks what's wrong. She pushes him away, then jumps into her father's small wooden boat moored at the dock. Larry grabs the oar from Alice, trying to stop her, and begs what's wrong. The boat moves away from the dock and he jumps into the cool waters and swims toward her, saying the tall brunette is his cousin from New York.

Alice leans over to help Larry into the boat, but the boat flips and she is hurled into the deep waters of the river. She reaches up to Larry but she can't see him. Holding her hand out, she goes down, her blue gown billowing out over the black water. Frantically, Larry screams for his beloved.

At the Palm Tree Yacht Club, the band is playing the last song of the night "Home Sweet Home." At 8311 Riverview Drive, the ocean breeze blows through the dining-room window, catches the wedding invitations and scatters them.

After reading Alice's story, never again will Jo and Cassie walk to the river or stand on the river bank without reliving Alice's fateful night a half century ago. They even think they hear Larry calling for Alice.

"She's in the house, looking for you," they say to him.

Sympathetic to the plight of Alice's life, nevertheless Jo and Cassie realize they can't do anything about it… and they have Cassie's wedding to plan. Because the war has just ended, although Cassie did finally find silk for her wedding gown, she has to settle for white-satin bedroom slippers for shoes. Then just as she is tearfully accepting that she won't have a wedding cake either, a large box of sugar arrives—hoarded rations from Ron's family in Georgia.

On October 12, 1946, Cassie and Ron are pronounced husband and wife at the Sandy Beach Methodist Church where they met. Six bridesmaids, each in a gown of a different color of the rainbow, look on. Ron's parents, Ella and Harry, are there, along with Aunt Hilda and Uncle Jim. The two women still cannot believe Ron is getting married.

Jo laughs merrily. "Welcome to the family. Ron is marrying into one of the best."

At nineteen, Jo is a beauty and a social butterfly. She catches the eye of Ron's younger brother, George, who is home from the war. George becomes Jo's knight in shining armor when he runs to the store for smelling salts after she swoons just before the ceremony, upset that her sister is leaving home.

*I will not think about Cassie leaving,* Jo then tells herself firmly. *Not right now anyway.* Jo has an idea that makes her feel better instantly. *Why not go to college in Georgia? Be near Cassie, be near George, get a great education in the meanwhile.* She won't tell her parents the education is secondary. Smiling, Jo hurries off to perform her duty as maid of honor.

The reception is at the house on Riverview Drive. There is no band. The war changed all that. However, the Ink Spots hit song "If I Didn't Care" drifts across the lawn from a radio while the bride and groom greet the guests.

This is a dual celebration. Hugh also proudly shows off his new wife, Mabel, and their young daughter, Faith. More fortunate than most, he spent much of the war stationed at West Palm Beach as a military photographer. One weekend he and Mabel married, not knowing when peace would return to the world.

Cassie is a beautiful bride, reminding Jo of the night she thought she saw Cassie in the mirror. She knows this moment will be over soon just like that fleeting reflection—except it isn't the lady in blue going away, it's her sister.

Cassie and Ron leave on their honeymoon. From the Smoky Mountains, they will go to Masseyville, Georgia, to live their new life together.

Jo has a talk with Alice. "It's just you and me, girl. At least until *I* can get to Georgia, too."

# BOOK TWO

### *Noel*

*The ghost in man and the ghost that once was man*
*Are calling to each other in a dawn*
*Stranger than earth has ever seen.*

—Alfred Lord Tennyson

# CHAPTER 10

*How do I love thee?*
*Let me count the ways.*

## 1955
## Shady Hill, Florida

At four years old, I know enough not to find myself the odd girl out at my grandparents' house. Whatever the sleeping arrangements, I will be bunking with another living, breathing, human being. Even at this young age, I sense the presence of an extra someone in the otherwise empty rooms. I run through the freezing cold spot of the dining-room doorway—even in mid July—knowing I am sharing the opening with an unseen someone who is also passing through. I stop and look, convinced I should see someone, but no one is there.

Mama Cason's household runs a little differently than ours at home in Georgia. After supper, she closes the kitchen, although she feeds us so good at mealtime that I don't really miss the nighttime snack.

Noel Brock

After dark on summer nights, the whole family gathers on the front porch, rocking and talking. We watch the orange-glow moon and the stars illuminating the Halifax River. It suits my six-year-old sister, Jen, and me to stay with the large group.

Mama Cason likes to hear "ole blue eyes" as she calls Frank Sinatra. As always, the house lights are out. Her electricity bill is not only nine dollars without a very good reason. Besides, in the open house with the salty breezes, it is cooler with the lights off.

Jen and I also don't have to worry about being in a room alone. We watch *Gunsmoke* on TV and I watch the old grandfather clock in the room beyond the porch. Never again will I go alone to the other parts of the house at night, nor pass the living room or dining room.

By the time I am six years old, the invisible houseguest on Riverview Drive has a name. I overhear my mother, Cassie, and my Aunt Jo talking about Alice. Then a lot of things begin to make sense, like the nightmares my mom has whenever we go to Shady Hill and she screams that someone has touched her. This never happens at home.

One winter night while visiting my grandparents, my dad, Ron, hollers out, saying something grabbed his foot and pulled him to the end of the bed and he nearly fell off. My mom woke up as he sailed past her in the bed. Now he is a true believer in Alice.

Mama Cason, a beautiful southern belle, has always cared about what the neighbors and friends think about everything. I can't even yell when I romp outside or play the television too loud. She also

## The Lady in Blue

doesn't broadcast her ghostly visitor. Very few people are told about Alice, although some folks probably leave the house wondering about a few things.

As a child, I have few answers as to why the silver tea service, tray and all, crashes to the floor in the middle of the night, leaving an empty spot on the dining-room buffet; why the floors creak and my bed squeaks, why the room fills up with a presence so intense that it doesn't matter that another person is sleeping beside me. Fear moves me closer to my sister, my bed partner. Then I sweat, because after Daddy was pulled out of bed by an invisible hand, even in the summer heat none of us sleeps with our feet out of the covers.

My love for my grandparents, though, overcomes my fear of Alice; and fun at the beach and in the large rambling house on summer days overcomes my nervousness. It's easy to forget the lady in blue when playing on the lush green lawn on a warm afternoon. The luscious grass and the smell of the citrus trees makes the yard a perfect playground. My summers at the coast are most enjoyable.

Our adventurous godmother, Jo, is delightful. My sister, Jen, and I think she must have hung the moon and the stars. Jo said she is our guardian angel. There is comfort in knowing that if anything happens to our parents, Jo will be our legal guardian.

Aunt Jo works as a civil servant at a nearby air-force base. The local auxiliary naval air-force station closed when World War II ended. Although she was too young during the war to work in any capacity except volunteer, it doesn't surprise her family or friends that she has chosen to work for the government. Her loyalty to the

Noel Brock

United States of America is apparent and she takes her *classified* assignments very seriously.

Aunt Jo is also loyal to her southern heritage. She may have been born a Floridian, but her ancestral roots trace back from the Irish in Charleston, South Carolina; and to a Cherokee Indian great-grandmother who married a deep southerner from Waycross, Georgia. Aunt Jo even looks a lot like Scarlett O'Hara, with her flamboyant, flirtatious and rebellious ways, reminding us all of the famous *Gone with the Wind* southern belle.

Besides being charming and beautiful, Aunt Jo is very brave. Jen and I decide that if Aunt Jo isn't afraid of our special guest named Alice, we won't be either. Then one night when I am ten and Jen is twelve, all that changes.

When everyone else is asleep, Jen and I slip out of bed—to see if we can see Alice. It's one a.m. We sit on the light-aqua sofa at the end of the long living room, and face the walnut cabinet with the rose bowl from Germany on the top of it. I am admiring this antique of my grandmother's when I smell a fragrance of lilacs permeating the air. Then a blue apparition slowly starts forming against the white wall. I grab Jen's hand, and we scream simultaneously and run to our sleeping Aunt Jo.

"It was a lady!" Jen exclaims.

I burst into tears.

Now wide-awake, Aunt Jo comforts us and listens patiently to our identical tales of a blue vapor that looks like a woman.

Jen and I are both distressed—not so much from fear, but be-

## The Lady in Blue

cause we have just blown our greatest chance to *see* Alice, the woman in blue.

# CHAPTER 11

*Life is good.*
*Life is fun.*
*Just a ghost*
*On the run.*

## 1958
## Shady Hill
### *Randy*

I am still seven and my little brother, Randy, has been born. Our trips to Florida become more difficult with three children but not less frequent.

By three years old, Randy is a most mischievous child, always exploring and into everything. He keeps the household up on a few occasions, to the delight of Jen and me. We are older and tired of going to bed at the ten-p.m. curfew. It is on these nights that my sister and I almost redeem our lost chance to see Alice: faint shadows on the walls, reflections in the dining-room mirror, unaccounted for grandfather-clock chimings. We are breathless!

On one trip to Shady Hill, Mama Cason shows us her new sofa-

## The Lady in Blue

bed in the new sunroom, a huge room that spans the backside of the house. With its red-brick tile floors, windows on three sides, and masonry fireplace, the room could be in *Southern Living* magazine. Now we eat our meals at the long rattan table in the sunroom instead of the dining room, which is perfect for our expanding family.

When Jen and I make up Randy's bed on the new sofa in the sunroom, I mutter, "*I* wouldn't sleep out here by myself."

"Shhh," she whispers. "Don't make him afraid or he'll come sleep in our bed."

Late that night, I wake suddenly and in a sliver of moonlight see Randy's red curls and freckled cherub face on my pillow. In the morning, with his green eyes wide, all Randy will say is, "Somebody came out there while I was sleeping and I didn't know her."

Jen and I have always told our ghostly experiences to Aunt Jo. Now she is leaving. She is getting married and leaving Florida. Mama Cason and Denny are also unhappy. Nothing is really wrong with Tim. He's just different from all the guys who were part of the Casons' lives during the war. Tim is tall and stoic, twelve years older than Aunt Jo, and divorced. These facts are hard for Mama and Denny to accept. That Tim is of German descent—only fifteen years post-Hitler—is even harder for them to bear.

Jen and I meet Tim when we go to stay with Aunt Jo at her duplex. When Uncle Hugh takes us to Sailor's Beach, Mama sends home-cooked food with us to Aunt Jo. Jo asks her handsome neighbor to drive Jen and me around in his Karmen Gia convertible; he strongly resembles Rock Hudson, the heartthrob of these days. He and Jo tell us his name is Tim Jeffries, but we are to call him Jeff… and Aunt Jo says we are not to mention him to anyone.

When Jen and I get back to Shady Hill, Mama Cason asks us if we ate the roast beef she sent.

"Not much at all," I say. "Some man named Jeff ate most of it."

Jen looks at me. *Oops.* I then realize that was exactly why Jo told us to call him by another name. It wasn't time for Mama and Denny to know about Tim.

"Jeff" loves us three kids—Jen, Randy, and me—and puts up with our antics. At Sebastian Inlet, he teaches us how to float on our backs. Uncle Hugh's two children, my older cousins, Faith and Rob, also think Aunt Jo's betrothed is exciting and that it's neat he works for NASA and knows all the astronauts.

I wonder, however, just how smart Tim can be. He helps put men in outer space, but he won't believe in Alice until he sees her? I know he's *heard* the lady in blue. On one of his visits he inquired about the whispering in the hallway all night, and I heard him ask my dad if he heard someone slam a door just before dawn. My dad laughed all day, saying Tim had seemed a little too sure of himself.

There is no doubt that unhappy families cause unhappy ghosts. There is a lot of bumping and knocking these days. Randy always feels a little strange in the house and tells us of falling objects and quick blue shadows on the walls. He prefers to sleep with us—his girls, as he calls us. The three of us feel safer together in the double bed… as long as we keep our feet under the covers.

Come spring, the time is finally right for Aunt Jo and Tim's wedding. After much planning for the event, the special day dawns bright and sunny, and the family gathers at Shady Hill at the same Sandy Beach Methodist Church where my parents were wed right after the war. Cassie is the matron of honor; Jen and I are junior bridesmaids.

"Jen, do you think Alice will come to the reception at Mama's house?" I ask while she is placing the tulle headpiece of tiny daisies on my head. I twirl in my white-and-blue chiffon ballerina dress and Jen tells me to stop because she can't fix my hair. "No, she hates weddings," she answers.

As always, the house and grounds are beautifully decorated, and the Casons give a great party after the wedding. Friends greet the happy couple, and Jo excitedly throws her bouquet. Faith catches the white roses and the crowd cheers.

Later, Aunt Jo and Tim leave 8311 Riverview Drive, bound for their new home in Huntsville, Alabama. Jo waves radiantly from their car window, and Mama Cason and I stand holding hands. As the 1960 Plymouth pulls out of the driveway, she lets go of my hand and wipes away a tear… and I wonder if Alice is the only one who hates weddings.

# CHAPTER 12

*Twas the night before Christmas*
*When all through the house*
*Not a creature was stirring,*
*Not even a mouse.*

## December 1962
## Shady Hill

Jen and I spend Christmas at the beach. All of our friends think we are so lucky to get to go to Shady Hill every other year for Christmas. We later learn that our parents have been taking the Santa presents for us three children, very industriously packing the loot in the back of the station wagon; one year we even got bicycles. We never ask questions, deciding it's best to assume that Santa Claus is bringing our gifts from the North Pole.

One Christmas Eve when everyone gathers in Mama and Denny's living room—my family, Aunt Jo, and Uncle Hugh's crowd—Jen and I are playing a new game, Candyland, with our cousins, Faith and Rob. Although older, they are always fun. Denny opens a present, a beautiful cashmere sweater. We laugh because he always puts

## The Lady in Blue

his gifts away as soon as he opens them, worried that several of our male relatives who also wear size *large* might take his stuff home.

All of a sudden there is a tap on the living-room window over the sofa. We all stop and look. In the dark of the night, we see only blackness. There is no moon and only a few stars. Then a tap on one of the glass panes becomes louder.

Faith screams," Look! It's Santa Claus looking at us!"

Very clearly we see the outline of a face. Personally, I don't see a beard, just a face, but I join in, "Santa Claus! Santa Claus!"

Ron and Hugh run outside to catch Santa and come back perplexed. Ron shakes his head, and Hugh says, "It *is* Christmas Eve, you know. Anything is possible."

Out of the corner of my eye, I see Aunt Jo and my mom exchanging a glance and raising their eyebrows… as I have seen them do so often here at Riverview Drive. The adults tell us that Santa must have wanted to come but couldn't since we are still awake and we need to go to bed. So, as soon as our cousins leave, Jen, Randy, and I obligingly go to bed. However, I am in tears. I am afraid it *was* Santa at the window… and I am afraid it was not. Faith said she saw a flash of red. *The lady in blue might not always wear blue,* I think.

Jen and I sleep with Aunt Jo and the couch under the window remains empty that night. In the night we hear footsteps and agonize over whether it is Santa or Alice. Never will we believe it is only Cassie.

# CHAPTER 13

*Tea for three.*
*Talk is free.*
*Tea for four.*
*Tell us more.*

**August 1963**
**Shady Hill**

Again this summer, Mama's next-door neighbor, Mrs. Whitman, insists on taking "Wanda's little granddaughters" out for tea at a fancy restaurant. Jen and I dislike the ordeal of dressing up, but most of all we dread Mrs. Whitman's driving. She is an accomplished pianist and maneuvers the accelerator just like playing piano pedals. We jerk all the way to town and our heads bobble. There's no air conditioning and we're hot. I laugh because we now have *our* family's first car with air conditioning and we are already spoiled. Jen doesn't laugh though. Her nylon crinoline is itching her legs and her pale-pink dress is sticking to the sweat on her back.

Mrs. Whitman chooses the Green Ives Tea Room. Jen and I politely sip our Lady Grey hot tea from the dainty demitasse cups and frown at each other: *How boring this is.*

## The Lady in Blue

Then the whole trip suddenly gets better. The waiter brings out chocolate cheesecake in warm raspberry sauce. While we are savoring the scrumptious dessert, Mrs. Whitman starts talking to us about Alice. Jen and I figure if a neighbor doesn't know, who does? So we listen and she tells us tidbits we have never heard before. Jen and I know Alice died at the house on Riverview Drive, but we don't know how or why.

Then we tell Mrs. Whitman about seeing someone at our living-room window. She gives us her theory and tells us the love story of Alice and Larry. Jen and I sit in awe.

Mrs. Whitman believes the fiancé Larry is looking in the window… and Alice is looking out. Jen and I close our eyes and visualize 1905 when Alice drowned in the river and Larry kept trying to find her. Now we are beginning to understand why Alice is so sad.

# CHAPTER 14

*Always believe what you know to be so.*

## 1965
## Huntsville, Alabama

Aunt Jo and Tim still live in Huntsville. This summer break, Jen and I are happy to visit them. Randy wants to come, but he has a Cub Scout camping trip already planned.

We have missed our godmother and tell her our latest Alice story. Excitedly Jen explains how once when Mrs. Whitman was visiting Mama Cason, the draperies in the dining room moved back and forth—but there was no breeze.

I add, "All of a sudden the room temperature dropped twenty degrees! Mrs. Whitman was horrified!"

"I don't have a new Alice story," Aunt Jo says, "but I do have something strange to tell you girls."

She and Tim were returning home from a business trip to Tennessee and driving through a bad stretch of mountainous roads. She was asleep in the backseat when suddenly she sat up and yelled, "Tim, pull over immediately!"

He thought she was sick and pulled over at the next shoulder beside the guardrail, then asked why they were stopping.

Jo was shaking. "We were about to be involved in a wreck."

After a few minutes, she felt calm again. "It's all right now. We can go."

Slowly he moved back onto the dark mountain road. As they topped the next incline and were starting over the other side, they saw something ahead and he slowed down. A white Impala had just passed them while they were parked beside the road. Now it was upside down. It had collided with a tractor trailer-truck that lost control on the treacherous hill.

Tim turned to Jo, clearly relieved. "A hug I give to you, my little psychic friend. You just saved our lives."

"So you finally believe me?" she said.

"I do indeed."

"And one day you will believe me about Alice, too?"

"I'm getting there," he said. "Yeah, I'm getting there. I'll believe anything you tell me for the rest of my life."

Aunt Jo pauses and smiles at Jen and me.

Several days later, Jen and I are reluctantly getting ready for our trip home to Georgia. Tim then tells us they have some exciting news. They are moving. He is being transferred to New Orleans and they have bought a century-old home in Mississippi right at the Gulf of Mexico.

## Noel Brock

Jen groans. "Oh. Our Jo is moving even further away from us."

However, I am thrilled. I have heard about the neat little sailboats near Biloxi and the calm water without the giant waves like in the Atlantic.

I notice that Aunt Jo seems a little sad though… like she is seeing the future and not liking what she sees.

# CHAPTER 15

*Summer after winter,*
*The times we share*
*Are precious memories*
*Beyond compare.*

## 1967
## Shady Hill
### *Mama Junior*

Turning sweet sixteen is great. Even better is the trip I get to take to Shady Hill by myself. Well, Randy is with me, but he doesn't count since he is only nine.

Mama Cason hugs me when I arrive and comments that Ron and Cassie know how level-headed I am.

"I still cannot believe they let me come by myself," I say.

"You're a good driver," my grandmother says. She also compliments my cooking. "I have heard from Masseyville what a good cook you are. They tell me they call you Mama Junior." She smiles broadly.

"You know I learned my culinary tricks from you," I say. "No one will ever compare to you… but I do have two weeks to learn more treats." I grin hopefully and she nods with pleasure. The real treat in store for me this trip, however, is not from the kitchen.

Randy insists on making a pallet on the floor beside my bed at night, because he refuses to sleep alone in this house. I really want Mama Cason to bunk with me and let Denny sleep with my brother. However, my grandparents are old-fashioned about their sleeping arrangements, saying they can list the nights in single digits they have slept apart during their married life. *No doubt,* I think. *If I lived in this house, I wouldn't sleep apart either.*

About midnight, the third night we are here, Randy wakes me up. "Sis, I think we have a visitor."

"What are you talking about?" I ask groggily.

"The closet door keeps opening and closing. It's hitting me in the head."

I urge Randy to find another place to sleep. "You know there's a vacant bed and two available couches in this house."

"No, you don't understand. There is someone in the closet." He's getting quite upset.

I groan and reach for the light switch—but before I can turn on the light we both hear the closet door open again and soft footsteps move away from us. I illuminate the room brightly and the bedroom door starts closing slowly on its own. By the time the door clicks shut, Randy is in my bed, holding my hand tightly, as if I have the answers to the spookiness of these nighttime hours. Little does he know that for sixteen years I have tried to figure out who and what Alice is.

## The Lady in Blue

There is no further cajoling on my part to get Randy out of my room that night, nor any of the eight nights that follow. In the morning, he tells our grandmother about our visitor and several other encounters he's had. She just smiles.

When driving home to Masseyville, I glance at my sleeping younger brother in the seat beside me. He's worn out from not sleeping well at night. He looks so peaceful, and I turn the radio down so he can get some rest. A few minutes later, he lifts his head. "Do you think that lady will ever go to heaven?"

# CHAPTER 16

*I send my prayers through time and space,*
*Your soul to take by His great grace.*

## May 1971
## Shady Hill, Florida
### *Denny*

My grandfather Denny Cason is dying. Cancer has ravaged his body and he has only a few months to live. He has teased us, played with us, and made us laugh. We love him.

A short stocky Irishman, he walks with a slight limp. He laughs about when his brother accidentally shot him in the foot, then put him in a wagon and rushed him to town. His brother later became a doctor.

Denny can tell a joke like no other. First, his powder-blue eyes start to twinkle, then he starts to talk. By the time he gets to the punch line, he is laughing so hard that no one can hear the best part. But we are all laughing anyway—so contagious is Denny's happy mood.

## The Lady in Blue

His spirited personality definitely accounts for the host of people at Shady Hill and surrounding towns who call him friend. Jen, Randy, and I call him Denny, defending our right to call him by his first name. "But, Mama, that *is* his name." Cheerfully, our grandfather says to call him whatever we want... as long as we call him. Yes, it is easy to love our Denny.

I have been feeling for days that a tragedy is about to occur. I just don't know what or how.

When I come home from college this weekend, my mother is crying. "The cancer is back," she says. "Your grandfather won't be with us very long."

We all go to Shady Hill to spend time with Denny. He reports that as he walks the house at night, he has company. Alice walks with him, sits with him, even speaks to him. He doesn't tell us everything. He is a quiet man about things of the heart.

It gives us comfort that besides Denny's profound religious beliefs supporting him in his final days he has a familiar presence with him—a good Methodist and his friendly ghost, together in the cream-colored Queen Anne recliner under the archway, which replaced the infamous platform rocker that rocked every night for the decade before it.

Then Denny is in the hospital. Wanda walks into his private room. "Hello, darling."

Even comatose, he opens his eyes for the girl he has loved since she was fifteen and he seventeen. I am overwhelmed at their timeless spaceless love. Mama Cason holds her Denny and he passes into eternity. A little piece of her soul goes with him… until the rest will follow.

Our family eventually goes to the house that Wanda and Denny shared for thirty-four of their fifty-six years together. That night, we hear familiar footsteps in the hallway. Just Alice's. Denny isn't walking around in pain anymore. Then we hear the doorknobs rattling on each bedroom door in succession: Alice comforting us in the only way she knows. I think of the love I witnessed today between my grandmother and grandfather, and the other love so powerful that a young girl is still searching for her missing love.

I am sleeping alone in the sunroom. With the house full of family members, the pullout sofa-bed is my only option. My fiancé, Frank, has gone to a motel with my brother, Randy.

Everything is fine until three a.m. when a loud boom startles me awake. In the moonlight, I see a large book on the floor. It fell off the middle of the round end-table. The book holders are still holding up the other books. There is only an empty space in the middle. In my white nightgown, I jump to my feet, arguing with myself. *Girl, you know you did not just see that.*

The white, wooden rocking-chair in the sunroom is rocking fast and furiously, the chair my mom used to have in her bedroom. I remember her telling me that when it rocked, she usually had *company* coming. *I do not wish to have anyone visit me!* I think with commanding.

I quietly raise the window into the nearest bedroom and climb

## The Lady in Blue

through. My sister, Jen, and her husband, Ethan, shoot straight up in bed, thinking I am Alice.

"What is going on here?" Ethan asks. "Never mind. Don't tell me," he answers himself, then pulls the bedspread up over his head.

By now, all three of us are wide awake and all three of us are in the double bed. I lie there thinking that maybe the next time I come to Shady Hill, I too will be married. Eventually, sleep comes to us; and we are grateful, for by now we are all holding hands.

The next day, Frank and I return to Georgia, because my college final exams are pending. Jen and Ethan remain at Shady Hill another night. Grandmother moves them to the bedroom next to the dining room, but Jen can't sleep. She feels the mattress go down and someone sitting on the foot of her bed, then her legs being rubbed up and down in a comforting motion. The moonlight glistens on the mirror and dances around. In the brightness of the room, Jen sees no one on the bed besides her sleeping Ethan, but the stroking continues. She buries her head and moves closer to him and wills herself to sleep. Then she dreams she is face to face with Alice, reaches out for Alice, and Alice slowly backs away until she disappears into shadows.

# CHAPTER 17

*When slumber comes, it is too late.*
*The cool night breezes will have to wait.*

## 1973
## Shady Hill, Florida
### *Frank*

The house isn't the same without Denny. My grandmother no longer lets the breezes from the river blow through open windows at night. She keeps everything closed. The house is so hot that I feel like I'm smothering, and the damp sheets stick to my body.

Mama is afraid. Frank (I'm married now) laughs that she is afraid of outside creatures but lives everyday with a ghost who frightens the bravest of men into submission. Of course, Frank does not fear Alice—but he hasn't met her yet. "Your day will come," I say.

That night, I hear Alice walking around in our bedroom. Frank is asleep and doesn't feel Alice brush his foot—which is sticking out from under the sheet. I believe that those who are not receptive to Alice do not experience her as readily.

# The Lady in Blue

Frank and I take Mama Cason to her church, then to the Grouper Delight Restaurant, then to the beach. She tries to be a good sport, but we see how much she misses Denny. We finally convince her to open the porch windows and we all sit in the glider, enjoying the breeze and watching the sunset over the river. I love being with my grandmother.

For our trip home to Masseyville, Mama loads a snack—as she calls it—ham and cheese sandwiches, into our ice chest. She doesn't look at me because her eyes are tearing up. "Tell Cassie to hurry down to see me," she says. " I know Hugh and Mabel want your mom and Ron to go with them to the Beachwood High School event in June. Some of their old friends can't wait for the reunions to get together."

I hesitate, then ask, "Mama, are you afraid to stay in the house alone?"

"No child," she says. "My life and my memories are in this old house. I sit on the porch in my glider, rocking to the tune of each life verse and the tempo of each life song as the sun sets over my very own river. Every good chapter replays over and over in my mind. The sad ones, I just erase. I will never leave this house."

Frank and I pull out of the driveway, and I look back at Mama Cason. She is still a beautiful woman. Standing erect, with her apron blowing around her, she waves goodbye and I think of Alice who also will never leave this house.

# CHAPTER 18

*She is the spirit of air,*
*A flicker of light,*
*The hope of tomorrow,*
*The star of night.*

## 1975
## Shady Hill, Florida
## *Cami*

My mother doesn't listen to me. Several months after my daughter, Cami, is born, she and I visit Mama Cason at Shady Hill. Mama cries when she sees Cami. Only three months old, my tiny dark-haired doll has perfect features. The famous dark Carr eyes, Mama's side of the family, are emerging, though for now they are still navy pools.

Sleeping is not one of Cami's favorite activities and Mama remarks how tired I look. My mother, Cassie, insists that I sleep in a separate bedroom so I can get some rest, that she and my new baby will stay in her old room. So I find myself sleeping alone—something I promised myself I wouldn't do.

At about five a.m., I waken, to a presence more than a noise.

# The Lady in Blue

Someone is rubbing my shoulder and my back. I flip over, expecting to see Mama Cason. What I see makes me freeze in place: in the early light of dawn, a long slender female arm, long slender fingers, manicured red-polished nails. No body. I hold my breath for a long time. Then I realize I'm all right. Alice would never hurt me. She has probably touched us all. After all, there are four generations of Carr women under this roof. And then there's Alice.

# CHAPTER 19

*Even though I am free to roam,*
*Give me back my home sweet home.*

## 1977
### *Aunt Jo*

Aunt Jo is divorced. There were some happy times in her marriage, particularly when she was living in the antebellum house in Mississippi. That *Gone With the Wind* type of home was perfect for a ghost, although they had none.

At first, the social whirl of NASA and New Orleans brought Jo and Tim closer as a couple. Then the pressure of his career and Jo's health problems began a downward spiral. After ending their marriage, she sold the white-columned home facing the Gulf and headed back to the east coast that had always been home for her. Once again she would work as a civil servant.

Back at the Cape Kennedy area put Aunt Jo within hours of her mother's house at Shady Hill, who would be glad to have her back even if only on weekends. And don't forget Alice. Nearly every Fri-

## The Lady in Blue

day, Jo drives from her ocean-front condominium to Shady Hill to visit Wanda.

Aunt Jo, our family's closest thing to a psychic (she senses rather than predicts), often calls me in Masseyville, asking who is sick or distraught or has had a fender bender. Usually she is right. It must be a Carr trait to have some "sight."

Mama Cason has also had several experiences in her lifetime. One night she woke up knowing Hugh had wrecked his truck. When delivering oranges to Deland, he had indeed turned over in a ditch. Mama even told Denny exactly where to find their teenage son.

Once Jo went to a famous haven for psychics close to Ocala, Florida, to find answers about Alice. One of the psychics at Cassadaga told Jo to "watch the woman who looks over your shoulder. She will always be with you."

I decide that the same senses developed for extrasensory perception are the ones that connect a person to a spirit, and maybe that is why Jo and Alice are connected—really connected.

One Monday morning when Jo drives back from Shady Hill to her job at the Cape Kennedy Space Center, one of her co-workers warmly teases her. "I thought you said you would never carpool, even the Share-a-Ride Campaign?"

Jo retorts that she would not, and several of her fellow workers challenge her. "Well, who was the woman riding in the car with you this morning?" They describe a pretty but old-fashioned looking woman with her hair up in a bun.

Jo just smiles. "Oh, yeah, I forgot about my friend, Alice." But, inside, Jo is horrified. She didn't know ghosts liked to travel, and she hopes Alice plans to return to Shady Hill. *Oh dear. How will she get back there?*

Jo just thinks the week has started out badly for her. Then Leigh, one of her condominium neighbors, comes by to see Jo for a second time.

"Why didn't you come to the door?" her neighbor asks.

"Sorry, Leigh, I went to dinner at the Ocean Grill in Vero Beach."

"And you didn't take your company?"

"Company?" Jo asks perplexed.

"Well, there was the prettiest dark-haired girl sitting in your Queen Anne chair by the rattan pagoda. I could see her through the window. That's why I thought you were home. She turned and smiled but wouldn't come to the door."

Jo sighs. "Leigh, you want to come in for a cup of coffee? I don't want to be alone tonight. I promise you, it will be a night to remember."

# CHAPTER 20

*Sing the "Song of Shadows,"*
*Play "the Spirit Song,"*
*Dance the evening melodies,*
*Pray the whole night long.*

## January 1982
## Shady Hill, Florida
*Mama Cason*

My vibrant grandmother, Mama Cason, died last night. But she was gone from us before her death. Her mind slipped away, leaving only her body. Her black eyes still danced sometimes, crinkling in a smile. It was hard seeing her like that, harder still to walk back into the home place on Riverview Drive after the funeral, knowing she will never return. The house seems so empty… or so we think.

My family has grown to four. Cami is seven; Lane is two years old. My sister, Jen, her husband, Ethan, and son, Dave, are here; as are my brother, Randy, and his wife, Paula. My parents, Cassie and Ron, have arrived with Aunt Jo. We assemble in the living room and discuss sleeping arrangements. With three bedrooms and several sofas, there is ample room for all of us to stay here.

Suddenly the grandfather clock chimes six times. We all look at Jo, then at my mom, Cassie. Not that the clock's time is a little off. It's just that a few minutes earlier, they were lamenting that the clock is missing its chimes and all of its working parts. It's empty.

We all decide Mama Cason must have left the parts at a clock shop for repair. However, the next day we find that the interior parts are at a jeweler's.

No one in our family wants the empty grandfather clock; so my mom, Cassie, agrees to take it—although with much trepidation. She already has endured a lifetime of looking over her shoulder.

That evening, Mama Cason's house gets colder and colder. It *is* January, we decide, and even in Florida heat is sometimes needed. My father and Frank go outside and look at the central heating unit. It seems to be all right, but the unit won't come on. Then a door slams and the *empty* clock chimes again… seven times.

Randy and Paula jump up and announce they are going to a motel. Everyone quickly follows and heads to the Ramada Inn. Everyone except Mom, Dad, and Jo who go to Aunt Kelly's in the next town.

The next morning, mom's brother, Hugh, sends a heating-and-cooling service to the house. When the repairman flips the controls ON, heat flows out. My dad pays for the unnecessary trip and mutters to them about strange things.

Later in the year, Frank and I go back one last time to Shady Hill,

## The Lady in Blue

to bring back to Georgia some items and furniture for my mother. She gives me the white-oak dining-room set and the infamous silver tea service, along with a few other small items to remember Mama Cason and Denny. The grandfather clock, still empty of its parts, goes to my mother's house. The diamond engagement ring, which once belonged to Alice, also goes to Georgia.

While Frank, Aunt Jo, my mom, and I clean the empty Riverview home we discuss the future of our family ghost. Will she stay with the house and the new buyer? Or will she feel her work is done and go away?

I want Mom or Aunt Jo to buy the house and keep it in the family. Mom says, "I haven't had a good night's sleep in that house in years. Why would I want to buy it?"

Jo says to Cassie, "If I could afford to pay you and Hugh your portion, I would keep the house. I'm not afraid of Alice."

My mom laughs. "If we *gave* you this house, you wouldn't stay here for long."

Frank agrees with my mom; and I know he is glad *we* don't live in Shady Hill, because I might want to buy the house myself. I love my memories of Mama Cason and Denny—more than I fear the memories of Alice.

The house takes nearly two years to sell. Could it be that Mama Cason's discretion did not work and it is well known that this is a haunted house?

Finally, it sells… to some folks from the North.

# CHAPTER 21

*A magic show of shadows,*
*Soft music in the night,*
*A touch on the shoulder*
*Much to my delight.*

## January 1998
## Masseyville, Georgia

The sixteen years since Mama Cason passed away have been busy ones. Cami has graduated from college and is married. Lane is eighteen and in a local college while still living at home. I am the director of an ancillary department at our large county hospital. Frank is a contractor. We moved into our present Georgia house in 1990, on land that has been in his family for one-hundred-fifty years. The wooded acreage is very private and quiet. The house is a typical brick-Tudor with a full basement, bringing the square footage to 4,700. Lane has the large "suite" downstairs. This house is absolutely nothing like the home I loved in Shady Hill.

My favorite room is the dining room, where I put Mama Cason's white-oak dining set and it reminds me of Shady Hill every time I walk by. My next favorite room is the living room, which I decorated

## The Lady in Blue

with the Ficks-Reed rattan furniture from the antebellum house in Mississippi. In these two rooms are mementos of the beloved house on the Halifax River. Sometimes the delicate butterfly music box or the white porcelain swan takes me on a journey decades back.

Aunt Jo and I are still very close and talk frequently on the phone; and she visits from Orlando as often as possible. We remember the good times at Shady Hill and we laugh about our Alice encounters. There are also still times when she feels Alice's presence in her Orlando house—as if Alice is trying to communicate with her.

For Christmas last year, I gave both Aunt Jo and my mom an oil-painted print of the house at Shady Hill. We all still feel connected to the old home place. And we still wonder about Alice.

# CHAPTER 22

*Enter this home with a happy heart.*
*When did all this chaos start?*

## October 7, 1998

This day starts out strange. At seven a.m., I put my slice of bread into the toaster and push it down. Frank has already left, and Lane is out of town. I run into my bedroom and dress for work, then hurry back to the kitchen where I smell something burning. The toast has burned to a black crisp and is stuck halfway down in the toaster. The toaster is still smoking and soot is everywhere! Then I notice that the cord is unplugged from the wall and thank my good fortune that Frank came home for something.

After work, when I walk into the kitchen alone, the small TV on one of the counters turns itself on, then off. I look at the microwave, a sure sign of a power surge, but there are no blinking lines. So I walk out of the kitchen… and the TV comes back on. *Well, I know there has to be a plausible explanation,* I think, *or I am losing my mind.*

## The Lady in Blue

Then I see my missing cordless phone in the top kitchen cabinet right beside the extra mustard and I really start to wonder about myself. Then I hear a crash in the living room, rush in and find a broken lead-crystal vase on the carpet. The problem is… I'm the only person in the house.

When Frank gets home at eight p.m. after a long day at work, I tell him about my day. He informs me that he did not come back this morning, and he did not unplug the toaster. I say a prayer. *Thank you, whoever is watching over me.* I know who.

# CHAPTER 23

*Oh, that you would believe it!*
*How can I say what I've seen?*
*Oh, that you could hear it!*
*How can I say where I've been?*

## October 30, 1998
## Masseyville, Georgia

Like any woman who has been in a house eight years or so, I decide to spruce up a few things. I start by refinishing the dining-room table, china cabinet, chairs, and buffet. The white-oak dining set has darkened since I brought it to Georgia.

The antique company estimates a refinishing time of two months. On October 29, the furniture leaves and my dining room is temporarily filled with boxes of my wedding china, crystal, and silver.

Taking the opportunity of Holbert Jeweler's annual October silver-refinishing sale, I also take the Shady Hill silver tea service to be re-silvered, although leaving it at the jewelry store makes me anxious because the service has a lot of memories associated with it. *If only the teapot could talk.*

Saturday night, I am reading alone on the sofa in the living room,

## The Lady in Blue

waiting for Lane to return home. Even at his age, I like to know when he comes in. Suddenly, I hear my boxed china and crystal rattling... as if someone is setting a dinner table in my unfurnished dining room. There is no table. There's nothing in there but boxes... and I am the only person awake in the house.

The clanging gets louder. I'm afraid to move, but I carefully get up and sneak toward the doorway. I see all the boxes, and the room is otherwise empty, so I return to the sofa.

Then a crash *outside* sounds like Lane has driven through the wall! Except that our white bulldog, Dolly, is still sleeping out there on the porch.

The next day, I tell Frank and Lane, "There is a familiarity about these strange happenings. Lane, remember me telling you about my grandmother's ghost?"

He nods. "Well, I think she might be here."

"Sure," he says cynically.

"This all started when I made the arrangements for the dining set to be refurbished. There's a relationship with Shady Hill and these bizarre happenings."

Frank reminds me that there is an old Indian burial ground on the back of our acreage, so how can I be so sure our guest isn't local?

"You really think an Indian would set an imaginary dining table with china and crystal?" I ask.

They start laughing.

# Noel Brock

"One of you stick your feet out of the covers tonight," I say with a chuckle. "That will prove my point."

# CHAPTER 24

*At some time in your life,*
*Someone's past sorrow*
*May come to haunt you.*
*Take it in stride.*

## November 6, 1998
## Masseyville, Georgia

The next week, Frank is walking through the dining room with me when a loud crash of glass *sounds* in the room. "There it is!" I scream. "*This* is what I was talking about!"

Frank mutters, "Well, if you would quit kicking the boxes of crystal." He knows I haven't touched the boxes. He's just uncomfortable with our new guest and isn't ready to accept that Alice has come for a visit.

"She seems angry about something," I say. "Maybe she doesn't like the dining set being gone or refinished. Maybe I shouldn't have taken the tea service to Holberts? Or is she trying to tell me something else?"

I could attribute these strange happenings to many different

## Noel Brock

things—coincidence, imagination, bad luck—but I hold out for Alice. Sixteen years seems like yesterday.

The night I know for sure Alice is really in my house, I'm watching television and I start sneezing. *Now* it is unmistakable: a heavy scent of lilac. "No! This cannot be!" It's been thirty-seven years since this same sweet odor saturated my young nostrils in Mama's living room, and I never forgot it.

# CHAPTER 25

*One day she left the seashore*
*To the hills to go,*
*Arriving with a slamming door,*
*Filling their lives with woe.*

**December 7, 1998**
**Masseyville**

My birthday celebration is early because I'm having surgery on my birthday. I'll be out of work four weeks and I don't look forward to extended time home by myself, which is unusual because I've always thought myself as great company… at least in a quiet and peaceful house. However, with the Alice circumstances of these last months, I don't want to be alone. It's like the old days.

Rattling continues in the dining room. When I walk through the room, my hair blows straight up, as if sucked up by an attic fan—and there are no fans of any kind in that room.

One night while Frank and Lane are visiting a friend at the hospital, I'm standing in front of our picture window when I hear footsteps behind me and feel hot breath on my neck. I turn, expecting to see Lane trying to scare me, but no one is there. Now, that's an experience that makes one tremble.

Frank is doing the grocery shopping during my recuperation. One afternoon close to Christmas I'm listening for his return when I hear grocery bags opening and closing and what sounds like cans and jars hitting the countertop. Thinking Frank is back, I call out. "Honey, do you need some help putting things away? Honey?"

When I get no answer, I ease myself slowly to the kitchen. Everything is the way Frank left it and there is no Frank.

Other days, I hear footsteps in the attic over our bedroom. Another time my name was called out loudly and echoed throughout the empty dining room. *Noel... Noel...*

I can't say I am not afraid. I am. And I *am* questioning why Alice has come to Georgia.

I'm also starting to question spirits in general, good spirits versus bad spirits. My daughter, Cami, is very concerned. She thinks any spirit inhabiting a home is evil. I tell her I know good people with haunted houses. Did I say haunted?

*Paranormal activities at my grandparents' house is one thing,* I think, *but this is my house. Why now? Why here? Why me?*

# CHAPTER 26

*Here she comes again...*
*Like bluebells in the rain.*

## December 25, 1998
## Masseyville, Georgia

My mother and father live three miles away. On Christmas Day, our entire family gathers at their house—aunts, uncles, cousins. Glad to finally get out after my recuperation, I am having a great day. The only person missing is Aunt Jo. She's had no children of her own and always spent the holidays with us, but not this year. She's been ill. Several different ailments have been bothering her. I miss Jo. Especially this year. I need to talk to her about Alice.

Instead, I'm talking to Jen and my mother over Christmas dinner when the burglar-alarm company calls and reports that our alarm is going off and Sheriff's deputies are on their way to our house. Frank and I rush back to our house where a deputy is in the backyard, scared to go into the fenced in area where the pool is because of our bulldog.

Noel Brock

An open window in the living-room has activated the alarm. However, it couldn't have been open when we left or the alarm wouldn't have armed. It activated three hours *after* we left home.

The deputy cannot believe that any thief would choose a window right beside a bulldog, and he is amazed that the window hasn't been damaged in any way. I want to tell him the problem can't be solved by law enforcement, but I don't. This is my problem.

# CHAPTER 27

*Sometimes you do what you are afraid to do.*

## January 2, 1999

The dining-room set is back. I joyfully unpack my boxes and carefully replace the crystal in the china cabinet. In the middle of one of the boxes, I find a goblet still wrapped in tissue but broken into a million shattered pieces. Then another. All the pieces wrapped in tissue *around* the shattered ones are still intact. While this is strange, I no longer question anything. The silver set will be home next week.

I am intent on making Alice happy. It doesn't work for long. One night, Lane calls me at midnight from his private phone in the basement. "Get down here!"

He is so frightened when I arrive that he can't move. "Lane, I'm sorry," I say to my trembling son. "I never imagined Alice coming downstairs to your living area. But just think—you've seen her!"

He'd awakened to dark staring eyes and long, dark curls; a girl in a light-colored dress, standing over his bed and watching him sleep. When he came fully awake, she ran out of the room. "I think she was a child," he says. "She wasn't very tall."

"Good try. Alice is only five feet."

He begs me to give the dining-room set away or sell it, hoping Alice will leave with the furniture. Frank's mother, Madge, offers to switch dining sets with me, referring to all the "confusion" at our house and inferring that a ghost would never go to hers.

I realize she's probably right. Madge and Frank are a lot alike, shaking their heads at my "much ado about nothing." They prefer life uneventful and mundane.

"No thanks," I say to Madge. "I just spent several thousand dollars to refinish this furniture and I'm going to keep it."

I laugh and tell Frank, "You would be bored without me. I have my very own lady ghost."

# CHAPTER 28

*I'm on the inside.*
*On which side are you?*

## February 1999

Lane and Frank are gone on a fishing trip and I'm here alone. I'm reading a book, reclined on the sofa, when the handle on the door to the deck starts rattling and visibly moves. I jump up, run to my cordless phone, and call my girlfriend whose husband is also on the fishing trip. I ask her to wait while I look out the door. The whole door is shaking. I look out the window. When I see Dolly, the bulldog, still asleep, I know who is knocking on my door.

Sharon offers to come over with her son, Bill, drive around back and shine their car lights onto the deck. I tell her, "No, that isn't the problem. It's not someone on the outside trying to get in." *It's someone already in,* I think. Sharon is relieved when I tell her not to come. I don't want to be here either.

To distract my nervousness, I call a college friend, Gayla. If anyone can make me laugh, it's her. Soon we are reminiscing about the old days and I feel much better. "The next time you're in Masseyville," I say, "come by and see me."

"I'll come soon, I promise," she says. "There's something I want to talk to you about, and I know you have experience. We think our house is haunted." She pauses, then laughs nervously. "Isn't that funny?"

I say goodnight to Gayla. Tonight is not the time to discuss her ghost.

In the middle of the night, I waken. Never a good thing when I'm by myself. I pull the covers around me and listen to the loud familiar tick-tock in my bedroom—intriguing since I don't have a grandfather clock.

I get out of bed and follow the sound to one of Frank's pocket watches on the chest of drawers. I pick it up and put it to my ear. The loudness of the ticking is almost deafening. My heart palpitates and my chest tightens, and I run back to the safety of my bed. The ticking stops, so I rush back to the watch, put it to my ear again and it sounds just like a pocket watch.

My sigh of relief is short-lived, however. Very softly—but distinctly—someone is calling my name. *Noel.*

# CHAPTER 29

*Kindred hearts*
*Sharing unspoken words.*

## February 14, 1999

Someone else might laugh, but I listen to every word Mrs. Jennings says. The young schoolteacher responded to my classified ad in the newspaper and is examining my wicker furniture for sale. She's searching for authentic old wicker for her antebellum home in nearby Chatham, Georgia. I imagine her beautiful old home close to the small town's college and smile. That's why I'm selling the wicker rocking chairs and loveseat. They belong on the front porch of a stately home that has white columns.

"The old Hunt place is lovely," Mrs. Jennings says, "but the best part is it's haunted." She waits for my reaction.

"Haunted?"

"Yes. The lights and water come on and off, and that's on a good day. Once my son got some helium balloons for his birthday and they danced all over his room." She looks at me and continues. "They were on the floor, then up on the ceiling, then in a chair. The three balloons sat in the chair for a while, then went to the floor again."

I listen and feel she senses my empathy. I take her story seriously.

"The best encounter," she says, "is the fire that started in the fireplace on its own."

This gets my attention. "What happened?"

"My husband was working the midnight shift, so I was alone in our bedroom. About three a.m., I wakened to an orange light glowing under the closed door. I jumped up, opened the door, and discovered a blazing fire in the fireplace. Two problems. It was July, and there was no wood in the fireplace."

For once, I am happy I don't have a fireplace. "Have you ever seen your ghost?" I ask.

"No, but the previous owners saw a young boy clothed in brown knickers on three or four occasions. He was coming down the stairway. Eventually, I expect to see him. I guess I'm hoping for the chance. Really, the situation is spooky, but I'm totally fascinated, and it makes for great conversation."

"I cannot agree with you more."

# CHAPTER 30

*Her thoughts are never far*
*As she wanders hither and there*
*From the beautiful old house*
*And the infamous rocking chair.*

## March 1999

Lane's girlfriend, Allison, has heard about our ghost. After the night a pencil came flying off a table at her, she always looks over her shoulder when going through the dining room. Lane laughed it off as just one of those things.

Another night, she was downstairs when she saw a blue shadow moving through the doorway and blocking the frame. She squeezed her eyes shut and ran into the next room and immediately wanted to go home.

I'm excited because she has *seen* something blue.

One night when Frank is out of town, I go to dinner with Lane and Allison. When we return, we stand in the kitchen, talking for an hour or so. Suddenly we hear a loud noise from downstairs, like a gush of water. We rush to the laundry-room door and see the water faucet on full blast in the utility sink. It couldn't have been left on accidentally. The stopper is still in and only a few inches of water are in the sink; it's only been running a few minutes.

"Who turned on the faucet?" Lane asks excitedly, hopping around. He always gets hyper when he's nervous. Allison is shaking.

*Why am I not hysterical?* I wonder.

I wonder if Alice is jealous of Lane's girlfriend. Something about their ages tugs at my memory. Alice and her fiancé were nineteen. *Allison and Alice. Lane and Larry.* The coincidence of their names gives me a funny feeling.

Lane and Allison head out the door to his pickup truck. Her blonde ponytail bounces as she hurries away. She turns and looks at me with her aqua-green eyes, as if to say, *Be careful.* Lane also looks at me.

"I'm okay," I hear myself saying to my incredibly handsome young son; olive skin, black eyes, dark hair. *Just don't break someone's heart*, I think to him as his truck door closes. On their radio, Toby Keith is singing "We Were In Love."

I think of the other young couple and the hot August night, and the song I hear is "Careless Love" floating amidst the humidity and darkness.

# CHAPTER 31

*Memories of long ago*
*Are coming back to me.*
*The ghost on Riverview—*
*Not here in Georgia, too!*

**March 3, 1999**
***Ron and Cassie's house***

Early this morning, my mother calls frantically. "The clock on our mantle is acting strange."

"How so?" I just *think* I want to know.

The clock came from Shady Hill *before* my grandparents' death. It was an ordinary clock, not the grandfather clock that had scared us all. Mother had put this clock on her fireplace mantle in 1971. My brother, Randy, had a bedroom downstairs then and the clock chiming had bothered him, so Mom turned it off, using the key… and put the key away. The clock did not run for twenty-eight years. Until today.

Now the clock's hands are moving whenever Mom and Dad aren't present. They say it's had three different times already and has chimed twice. Without the key. The clock does not run *officially*.

# Noel Brock

Once the hands moved from eight o'clock to six-thirty and they wondered if it was going backwards.

Mom and Dad are unnerved. They creep into the room to catch the hands moving—but never see it.

"Ron, what are you doing?" Mom asks him.

He's in a curled position, feet on the stairs between the kitchen and den, head looking around the corner. "Trying to catch the hands."

She shakes her head. Her neat, silver-coifed hair, belies the fact that she just woke up. "You know those hands will never move while you're watching." She smiles and her eyes twinkle. "Besides, Amerson Jeweler's said that clock *can't* run like it is."

"I hope his advice was free or you just wasted your money."

One Sunday several months later, I stop by their house on my way to church. I plan to set up a video camera and focus it on the clock, to see the movement of the hands. *This is insane,* I think.

No one is home, but I have a key. When I go into the empty family room, I suddenly feel afraid. Taping might not be the best idea.

Then the *nonworking* clock chimes. I hurry out so fast that I almost fall *up* the two steps to the kitchen.

Somehow all this feels tied to Aunt Jo, like we're supposed to check on her. She's still sick. I call frequently, but tell Mom and Dad they need to go to Orlando to visit her.

One evening in late March, Aunt Jo calls them, and the clock starts chiming during the conversation. Dad holds up the phone up

## The Lady in Blue

so Jo can hear the chimes. She begs them to hurry to see her. At this point, they are happy to leave home.

When they depart for Orlando, the clock is chiming for the last time. They just don't know it yet. Alice is happy. Her message has been received.

Noel Brock

## CHAPTER 32

*Lacy dresses,*
*Long brown tresses,*
*Flowers in her hair,*
*Lingering scents in the air.*

**2000**
**Masseyville, Georgia**

My parents are happy to have a quiet clock after their three-month episode, but things have not been quiet at *my* house. One night while again reading on the sofa, I hear a loud crash in the dining room. When I run in, I find my briefcase, which I left on a dining-room chair, on the floor and its papers scattered all over the room. I pick up everything, wondering what caused the briefcase to fall off the chair—after six hours—and what has strewn the papers. I don't have to wonder of course. By now, I know the answer for the strange things happening on Kennen Road.

Lane comes in from his evening out and after a while goes downstairs to his room. I've fallen asleep again while reading. Soon Lane is shaking me, asking, "Why are you stomping around upstairs?"

## The Lady in Blue

Obviously, it wasn't me. He grimaces. "And why did you throw your briefcase and stuff all over the floor?"

*Oh, no. Not again!*

It's time to give Aunt Jo another call. She still isn't well, but I need advice about her buddy, Alice. Jo always makes me feel better. She's always been connected to Alice, and I am close to Jo, so I feel connected to Alice, too—who seems to be insisting on making my house her home.

We compare notes on Alice, then Jo asks me to assume her power of attorney and to be the executress of her estate if anything happens to her. She is still young and full of life, even at seventy-three. I can't imagine anything happening to my Aunt Jo, although I have come to realize that Alice is encouraging phones calls and visits, as if it is her mission to do so.

# CHAPTER 33

*Backdoor friends are best.*

## September, 2000

Aunt Jo calls me excitedly about her visitors last weekend, cousins from Georgia who went to Disney World and came by to see her. Lauren, Bill, and Jack chatted for a while in the driveway before coming inside. Bill is the blood relative; Lauren is his wife. However, Lauren attended college with Jo in Georgia and they always have fun reminiscing about their wild times. Bill was in the air force and loves to talk to Jo about the military because of her knowledge of the Hawker Hunter, F4 Phantom ll, and Jaguar GRIs.

On this trip, Bill follows Jo into the kitchen. She's used to his chattiness and only halfway listens. Suddenly she perks up. "What did you say?'

He repeats his question. "Who was the lady sitting at your dining-room table when we walked in?" When he doesn't get an answer, he continues. "I hated to be rude, but she wasn't looking my way so I didn't acknowledge her."

Jo searches the room but doesn't see anyone. "Where is she now?"

"That's the weird thing. When you left the room to get our Cokes, she followed you out. Her long brown hair was blowing like there was a fan on it, but there's no fan."

He stops speaking for a moment, then whispers, "It's that woman from Shady Hill, isn't it? Wow. Wonder why she's here?"

*Yes. Why?*

# CHAPTER 34

*Love surrounds us all*
*As she quietly walks the hall.*

## Christmas 2000

After Thanksgiving, Aunt Jo calls. She wants to come for Christmas but can't drive to Georgia; and she's melancholy, which is uncharacteristic of her. I tell her I'll make airline arrangements and pick her up at the Atlanta airport; however, she doesn't want to fly because of her vertigo. But she says she *has* to come… because this will be her last Christmas. Not wanting to believe her, I laugh. But I *do* believe her. She has an uncanny sixth sense.

We agree on an unusual plan. She will take the Amtrak train to Jesup, Georgia, a town two hours away. Frank and I will meet her there and drive us all to be with Cassie and Ron. Frank has a soft spot for Jo, too, and I especially love him for making such an effort to make this visit happen.

It's several days before Christmas. We have to wait a long time at the depot, because the train has been delayed by a snowstorm in

## The Lady in Blue

New York. Frank says we should have driven to Orlando for Jo, and he would have.

Aunt Jo has always stayed at my parents' house when she visits Georgia. However, on this visit she does come to my home for dinner in Masseyville. All of my family come, including Jen and Randy; and the event becomes a party for Brent, Cami's husband. He just graduated from college. Everyone is celebrating and having a great time. No sign of Alice. All is well.

Christmas Day is memorable, with family, friends, and the simple joys of the season. Aunt Jo loves her black-silk pajamas from my family, and she gives me a special music box she particularly wants me to have. The small white-porcelain angel plays "Memories."

Lane then laughs and asks Jo if she's heard his story about his quick exit one night. The last time Frank and I went to visit Jo in Orlando, Lane was alone and downstairs, talking on the phone to his cousin, Adam. When he heard bad weather approaching, he said to Adam, "Man, the thunder is loud. It must be storming."

Adam, who lives half a mile away, laughed. "No. I see stars and a clear sky."

Carrying the cordless phone, Lane creeped upstairs, then realized the *thunder* was actually someone running heavily back and forth on the hardwood floor in the hallway. He rushed out of the house and went directly to Grandmother Madge's house for the night, his grandmother on Frank's side of the family—the unhaunted family.

# CHAPTER 35

*Who is the fairest of them all?*
*Silhouettes of blue shadows on the wall.*

## March 19, 2001
## Orlando, Florida

That unsettling feeling is hovering over me. I hate when I have this sense of foreboding. Sometimes the cloud lifts, but I never realize where the burden is coming from. Hopefully that will be the case today.

When I get to work at the hospital this morning, there are many problems to solve. An irate doctor calls about a wrong order on a patient. I summon the employee involved and try to figure out what happened. In the middle of the confusion, I notice my mother's phone number on my desk-phone caller ID. Because she rarely calls me at work, I take the call despite the current personnel issue.

Mother is crying. "Jo is dead. Cardiac arrest."

My beautiful carefree aunt is gone. All I can think is she was right. Christmas was the last time we were all together.

# The Lady in Blue

How glad I am that I brought her here on the Amtrak, and that I've had so many phone calls with her.

*Thank you, Alice.*

# CHAPTER 36

*She lost her true love by night.*
*The burden she carries will never be light.*
*She searches for Jo's mourning kin,*
*The loss of her best earthly friend.*

## April 2001
## Orlando, Florida

A month after Aunt Jo's funeral, I return to her home in Florida for her belongings, so many lovely things, many antiques and valuables from Shady Hill. Some will go to my mother, some to my sister, Jen, some to my brother, Randy, the rest to me. Just what I need. More former Riverview Drive belongings in my house to make Alice feel even more comfortable.

However, to my surprise, for the first time in three years all is quiet and I realize Alice has been here in Georgia to tell me that Jo needed our special attention and love before she left this earth. When I hadn't listened to Alice, she temporarily moved to my mom's house and chimed the empty clock to make us listen to her.

I must admit, I appreciate the freedom of no nocturnal visits, electronic problems, or spirit stress. *Adios, Alice!*

# CHAPTER 37

*Something old,*
*Something new,*
*Something borrowed,*
*Something blue.*

## October 2001
## Kennen Road

Alice is back. I don't know why or for how long, but today she is here. When I come in the back door, to my dismay one of the two temple-rubbings from Thailand, gifted from Jo, is on the floor. The large picture of the orange, dancing figure had been professionally framed and hung on my dark-blue dining-room wall when our house was completed in 1990. After eleven years, the picture has *now* come off the wall, landing four feet away, face down… and no broken glass. So tonight I listen for slamming doors, footsteps in the kitchen, and other bumps. I hear the sounds and I feel Alice's presence.

Preparations are being made for my parents' fifty-fifth wedding anniversary. We are all happy that several Florida relatives are coming. Aunt Jo's absence will be pronounced and our hearts ache with remembrance.

For the anniversary party, Jen and I have made a videotape of our parents' life and we're excited to show the journey of their lives, complete with their baby pictures.

The dinner party is grand and the entertainment perfect. Everyone is happy to be celebrating the monumental occasion. World War II is on the VCR-monitor screen and Ron is in uniform. In the background, George Cohan is singing "Over There." Then Cassie is sitting in the famous platform rocker at the Riverview Drive house to lyrics from "If I Didn't Care." Behind their wedding photos, "Whither Thou Goest I Will Go" plays softly.

In the midst of the happiness, my odd feeling returns. Something is definitely wrong.

The following week, my brother, Randy, is diagnosed with cancer. *Not my baby brother!*

He has been feeling very tired since September. The first week in October, he discovered a large lump in his neck. He knew at the anniversary party that on Monday he would get a diagnosis, but he didn't want to worry our parents.

He has been given only a few months to live, and he lives them to the fullest, an inspiration to the terminal patients in the oncology clinic where he's getting his radiation and chemotherapy treatments. He talks about Shady Hill and Alice and asks me if I've seen her lately. At Christmas, he comes to my house and tells me, "She is here."

# CHAPTER 38

*Now I lay me down to sleep.*
*I pray the Lord my soul to keep.*

## January 2002

Snowflakes float down all day. The ground outside Randy's hospital room is white. The curtains are open and he's excited that it's snowing in Middle Georgia. He keeps his face turned toward the window.

His cute, blonde nurse, Penny, urges, "Why don't you put on warm clothes, go outside and be a kid again. Play in the snow."

Randy nods and agrees that he should. Nothing to keep him from leaving this room and doing whatever he wants… as long as he does it soon.

Organ by organ his body is dying. Nothing in his forty-three years has prepared him for how to comfort his parents, wife, sisters, and two young sons. "Take care of my family," he tells us. "And not to worry, my affairs are in order. Both kinds. The boys and Lisa will be provided for. I will be taken care of as well. I guess the benefit to knowing you're dying is you can prepare. No sudden trauma to rip your soul apart so that you're searching for the pieces into the next century… like some people we know." He smiles, and tears travel down his cheek.

Randy settles back on his white pillow. Strands of his thick auburn hair are just starting to grow back after his treatments and are curling in small clusters. I think of the time at Shady Hill when I woke and found him in bed with me and Jen. Randy's faith is greater than his fear.

It's time to cry again. We are all there when Randy takes his last breath. He was even able to take Holy Communion on Sunday; a minister came to the hospital for him.

Randy dies on Tuesday. We have lost two beloved family members in ten months. The sadness is overwhelming.

My mother, Cassie, speaks at Randy's memorial service, just as she did for Aunt Jo. This the woman for whom the graduation rules were broken because she was too shy to give a speech. Cassie holds up by great determination… and a power greater than she. For those of us left, we keep examining our roots and our connections, most of all our priorities.

In the middle of the night, I waken to someone standing over my bed. I sit up and feel a shoulder and arm brush me. I turn on the light. The only other shoulders in the house are on the other side of the bed, Frank sleeping.

Then I hear footsteps in our long hallway, moving softly away.

## The Lady in Blue

How a soul in obvious turmoil can attempt to comfort us mortals is amazing.

What am I talking about? This whole thing is amazing!

# CHAPTER 39

*Music to our ears,*
*A voice from the grave,*
*A message to hear,*
*A soul to save.*

## 2003

Ups and downs, happy times and some sad times for the family. Life goes on.

So does the occasional slamming door, unexplained electronic problem, or touch on my shoulder. Frank has come to accept Alice and hopefully forgiven me for my unusual extended family.

Over time, Lane has developed an understanding of the woman in blue, although lately he has been a bit annoyed when friends come over and are scared by her antics; the latest, a musical toy playing a tune on and off all evening during a cookout. Lane says no one touched the push buttons. "And the switch was *off* anyway."

One of his friends, Steve, tells me about a night when several of them were standing outside our garage and the light in my Durango came on when Frank and I were out of town. As Steve questioned

## The Lady in Blue

Lane, the light went off and Lane gave him a flippant answer. "Oh yeah, the Durango frequently does that."

Steve grins at me and says they all keep their eyes open now and their guard up when visiting Kennen Road.

I was gone on a business trip to Utah for a week another time and the burglar alarm went off on its own, alerting the security company and law enforcement. Frank was more than annoyed because the alarm had been armed for AWAY since no one was home. The setting activates motion sensors to detect movement *inside* from a prowler. The security company monitors showed that our alarm had gone off due to the motion detector in Lane's room. Frank knew it wasn't a prowler but he didn't tell the security officer or the Sheriff's Department. Later that day, the alarm went off again. This time the "motion" was upstairs. I think Alice doesn't like my being gone. I'm glad she didn't go with me!

The night I arrive back home, after the lights are out, Frank asks me why I'm pacing the floor. He hears the two boards near our bathroom creaking.

"I'm in bed," I say.

Over the years, my sister, Jen, has been amused by Alice's antics at my home on Kennen Road and our parents' home on Voight Road. It's taken nineteen years, but Alice has finally visited Jen!

Jen is divorced now and only her son, Dave, lives at home with her. Alice's nocturnal happening occurred in Jen's bedroom. The headboard on her bed slides back and forth to store books. The set is old… and came from Shady Hill.

# Noel Brock

At three a.m., Jen woke to an orange glow *inside* the pillow sham on the still-made other side of her bed. The casing is open-weaved and crocheted, and light shone through every hole. With a start, she jumped up and grabbed the pillow. A flashlight was in the pillowcase and turned *on*. The flashlight had been in the headboard behind the closed storage door. Jen brushed the incident off and went back to sleep.

In the morning, while cooking breakfast, she realized the bedroom clock was incorrect and she was an hour too early. Then, to her chagrin, she found that every clock in the house was set at a different time and she had no idea what time it really was. Alice's time!

My parents are now complaining of music coming from *inside* their den wall, and they have started watching the mantle clock again. Laughing, I predict that my guest, Alice, might move again. Jen threatens to "ghostbust" her home if Alice shows up one more time.

My bedroom ceiling fan has five lamps. Four bulbs burned out last week. Too busy to change the bulbs, I have ignored the dimness. I'm in the bathtub, which faces the bedroom, when bright light suddenly fills the whole bedroom. I jump out of the tub, dripping wet, grab a towel and run into the room. It is ablaze with light and all *five* bulbs are burning brightly again.

Still shaken, since I'm home alone, I go into the kitchen and flip on the light switch. All six bulbs in the chandelier blow out and I

## The Lady in Blue

am standing in total darkness in my wet towel. At the same time, a living-room lamp comes on. *Thanks for the light!* I say to Alice.

Lane's birthday is Wednesday. His new girlfriend, Anna, joins us for dinner at a seafood restaurant. Dessert and presents will be at Cami's house later in the evening. Lane and Anna go by Kennen Road to pick up the cake I baked. When they walk into the foyer, the light flickers on, then off, then on, then off again.

When they return with the cake, Anna announces that she wasn't surprised. "Everyone knows about Lane's ghost." Nevertheless, she won't go anywhere in our house without someone with her. And some of Lane's other friends won't come at all.

At some point during Lane's birthday party, again I think of *Anna and Alice, Lane and Larry*. Another coincidence? Sure. Just like Anna's long, dark hair and pretty dark eyes on her tiny five-foot frame.

I've been tempted to call for help about Alice over the years, anyone: exterminator, validator, sympathizer. A friend has suggested a ghostbuster. She's heard of one in Atlanta.

"If I do 'bust' my ghost with some fancy electronic-beeping equipment," I say, "what would it prove? I know Alice is here, and I know she is free to leave whenever she wants. One day she probably will, maybe on to the next generation of Casons." It reminds me of the song at our family's weddings, "Whither Thou Goest, I Will Go."

I remember Lane groaning when he was younger. "I didn't even know this lady."

Noel Brock

Well, Lane, you know her now.

## CHAPTER 40

*Before the morning dew is on the ground*
*The lady in blue is walking around.*

## October 7, 2003
## Masseyville, Georgia

It's been exactly five years to the day since Alice came to Georgia and Kennen Road. Coming home from work after an especially hard day, I'm thinking how grateful I am it's Friday. I take the newspaper into the living room and collapse into a side chair—which is uncharacteristic of me because I usually read the paper at the kitchen table.

I glance around the living room and smile at how great my angel collection looks in the new curio wall-cabinet. Suddenly, I freeze and I cannot believe my eyes. On the narrow wall behind Frank's chair, the pictures of Mama Cason's house at Shady Hill and Aunt Jo's antebellum house in Mississippi are both hanging very crookedly. But that's not what takes my breath away.

I'm staring now. Below the extremely lopsided picture of Riverview Drive, brown liquid is running down my white wall. Lots of brown liquid.

I run over to the picture and take it off the hanger. The two rubber tips on the back of this professionally-framed picture have turned to liquid… and the liquid is running down my white wall.

I run outside to Frank. "My grandmother's house is bleeding!"

Frank comes in, appraises the situation with patient humor, and announces that I have a problem. I start to cry, begging for an explanation for the sticky brown glob on my white wall. The drapes are drawn, the air conditioner has been on all day, the lights have been out, and the house is cool. In fact, as warm as it is outside, the house is *unusually* cold.

I scrape the wet, sticky brown lines off my wall. A brownish stain remains. I lay the picture face down with the rubber tips facing up. The liquid is still bubbling, and the volume of liquid vastly *exceeds* the size of the tips. Even Frank can't rationalize this away.

The next day I put the picture in a sack and take it to the frame shop where it was framed. The tiny rubber tips are still dripping. I receive quick service, no questions asked. The only thing the clerk says as she looks at me oddly is, "I put clear tips on this time."

*What is causing this phenomenon?* I wonder. *Could it be my grandmother's mahogany teacart that Jen brought back from Aunt Jo's?*

After two years, Jen just today had placed it in her dining room for the first time. On a hunch, I call Jen and ask the date that the furniture refinisher started on her teacart. I am not surprised at her answer. It was the day *before* the Alice antics in her bedroom.

## The Lady in Blue

But why take the anger out on *my* picture? My mother has an identical picture at her house on Voight Road. Her picture of Riverview Drive hangs in direct sunlight, but her picture is fine; her rubber tips are hard and perfect.

Jen does not try to understand. "Do you want the teacart?" she asks. I laugh because we practically fought over it two years ago.

I know that finding the answers to the haunting of Riverview Drive might help solve the haunting of my own home. I also know that since the events happened one hundred years ago, the search won't be easy.

To save a trip to Florida, I first call five title companies. All say they cannot find the requested information. Being scientific by nature, I want concrete evidence. I want answers.

The historical archives that Aunt Jo researched in the 1940s are no longer available, so I go to the courthouse at the county seat about an hour away from Shady Hill. All title transactions before 1990 are on microfiche and I have to manually search the transparencies. For a search, most counties in Florida require the name of the owner and the date; one cannot search by the address of a piece of property. I cannot locate the information by a direct search of my grandfather Cason, so I try a reverse search of possible owners.

I try all transactions for 1935-1940, even though my mom, Cassie, knows exactly when her family purchased the house. After hours and hours, I realize the information isn't located in the archives.

Although the details of Alice's story are embedded firmly in my

Noel Brock

mind, from the numerous times Aunt Jo told me while we sat on Mama Cason's porch glider, I've accepted that I won't be able to confirm the story she discovered in her own research.

# CHAPTER 41

*To know me is to haunt me.*
*To love me is to leave me.*

## January 2004

After reading many books about the paranormal, I have learned the difference between ghosts and spirits and confirmed that Alice is a ghost. Supposedly, spirits have been to the other side and returned to earth for some reason; while ghosts have never followed the light to the other side, because of grief, turmoil, or a desire for revenge. Spirits tend to float around; ghosts walk on the floor, thus the footsteps we hear. Spirits know they have passed away; ghosts do not know they are dead.

I understand Alice's fascination with Lane. The lady in blue thinks she is alive and appealing to him. I have decided not to tell Lane. He would move out for sure.

Everyone seems to think spirits attach to people; and that ghosts attach to people, things, and/or places. It is also assumed that spirits can visit multiple family members, but that ghosts cannot be in two places at the same time. I know that Alice is in Georgia most of the time now. I wonder if the times she is not here, maybe she has gone home to Shady Hill?

Both spirits and ghosts are purported to have a fetish for electrical items, running water, rocking chairs, and chiming clocks. Odors are often associated with ghosts, like a favorite perfume or flower. Thinking of all these examples at Shady Hill and Masseyville, I shiver.

# CHAPTER 42

*Lady with the blue dress on.*
*Oh, dear, now she is gone.*
*Lady all around this town.*
*Look at her, she's in a gown.*

## February 2004

February has always been an active month for Alice. I'm not sure of the significance for her, but the experiences are memorable for me. Lane also has memories of a February night that he spent eating his midnight snack in the laundry room after hearing his name called. While alone in the dark kitchen, he heard a soft feminine voice. *Lane... Lane...* It was Valentine's Day.

I'm looking forward to several days at home by myself to get some things done. Frank and Lane have announced they are leaving for the weekend, fishing as usual. They are excited to be trying out our new boat, a catamaran, bought especially for offshore fishing. They named the boat *Noel & Company* in honor of Alice and me. Lane said he tried to explain the insinuation of the name to one of his fishing buddies and ended up saying, "Never mind. You wouldn't understand." After they leave for the weekend, I make a list of chores I hope to accomplish. My days alone are fine, but the two nights are a disaster.

Friday night, I have a late appointment at work and I get home just as the phone is ringing. I answer it downstairs. While I'm talking, a toy in the toy box sings a song, the dryer door slams shut, and water drips in the laundry sink.

I hasten my conversation and hurry upstairs to my bedroom, where I try to get absorbed in a book; but all I can hear is a crackle, a noise coming from the kitchen. I trace it to the oven. The crackling is the noise the oven makes as it regulates the temperature. The only problem is the oven is *off*. After spending a long time checking this out, I finally open the oven door. The inside is hot, probably maximum temperature; but the coils are not red and the oven has not been on.

I finally call Jen for help, and find no sympathy. "She's never hurt you," she says. "Just go to sleep. It'll be better in the morning." This from the sister who said if Alice comes back, she'll get a ghostbuster.

Saturday night is even worse. I go to a movie with some friends. After I take June and Christy to their homes, I am stopped for speeding, which is mortifying. Fortunately all I get is a warning ticket.

At home, I'm getting ready for bed when I hear soft music from the living room. Then it stops. Followed by the loudest crash I have ever heard. My mom, Cassie, is always up at midnight, so I phone her. She says, "Inside Alice problems need to be handled differently than outside burglar problems."

# The Lady in Blue

I keep Mom talking to me on my cordless phone while I go into the living room and look for the object of the crash. Nothing is amiss. Shaking, I walk into the hallway. Suddenly, a small gift-shop Southwest airplane comes barreling along the floor… and stops at my feet, with its red lights blinking on and off. I go to where the remote is kept and find that it and plane are in the *off* position. The lights continue flashing at me as if saying, *Hi*.

All of this while my mother is on the phone with me. "Your Dad and I will come and pick you up," she says insistently.

I feel the need to leave, but I don't want to wait on a ride; and the image of speeding away from Kennen Road in my nightgown and being stopped again by Officer Ward keeps me from driving. One other thought keeps me at home: the bedroom on Voight Road, where I would sleep, is downstairs next to the den, next to the old mantel clock that chimes. So, I stay home.

On Sunday night, Frank gets a big hug when he returns.

*Sleep at last!*

# CHAPTER 43

*Surely there will be talk tomorrow,*
*Bringing me great sorrow.*
*Why can't she stay at home?*
*Always, always on the roam.*

## March 2004

Writing a journal about Alice's mischievous maneuvers is the only way to remember everything that has happened in our house. I print the fifty-page journal off my saved computer disk for my mom to read a few of my exciting events with her family ghost. When the pages print on my home printer, I am aghast.

"Lane, look at these pages! Words printed all over the pages! Some words that aren't even on the disk." All are incomplete sentences. Plus, symbols, bold, italics, and different fonts—Arabic, Roman, Gothic—that I didn't type.

"It must be this ink-jet printer," he says. "Try the disk at work and e-mail the attachment to your work address. Try it both ways."

The print attempt at my office at the hospital yields even more bizarre results; so I call Abby, my Administrative Assistant, to come

## The Lady in Blue

look. This time the pages print perfectly. She shakes her head. She knows all about Alice. "Just don't bring her to work with you."

It's too late. Delia, the department's education coordinator, tells Abby she's hearing things in my office when working late at night—like typing on the keyboard, papers printing—but when Delia looks in, she sees no one.

Miss Mady, one of the older housekeepers, does see someone. Late one night she saw a flash of a figure of a woman in my office… and left her vacuum running and the door open until someone came back with her. "They can fire me," said Miss Mady, "but I won't go back in there at night by myself." I had wondered why she started cleaning my area before I leave each day.

Also, when I am working late and all is quiet, overhead I sometimes hear the pharmacy robot moving around upstairs on the second floor. One evening, when I am at my desk and listening to the robot, Miss Mady and Abby rush in. Last night, another cleaning lady also saw a "woman" in my office. Miss Mady's eyes nervously sweep my room. "Soon, no one on the staff will be left to clean in here."

Abby and I laugh. A 2004 robot and a 1905 ghost are contradictory indeed!

# CHAPTER 44

*Take it from me,*
*It's no fun to be*
*A witness to tricks and play*
*All because of one bad day.*

## April 2004

"Joe, hey this is Noel. I'm going to be late this morning. No, actually it's my car."

"You sound a little stressed, Noel. Take your time," my boss assures me.

"Okay, thanks."

Actually, it's not just my car. I don't know what's going on this morning, but I can't seem to get to work. No Kenny Chesney number one on the charts "When the Sun Goes Down" to wake me as every other morning this week; and the alarm was set like always, especially because Frank was leaving early to meet a subcontractor about a piece of land he is clearing.

When I can't find my badge or beeper, I just think it's normal morning stuff. Even when the microwave clock is wrong, I just think

# The Lady in Blue

I'm late. But when I find my briefcase contents strewn everywhere, I get suspicious.

Then I press the remote for the garage door to go up, but it stays down and the other door goes up. After twenty frantic attempts, I get out of my Durango and try the keypad. When I step out of the car in the garage, thick smoke greets me and I can't see or breathe. Blind and gagging, I fumble for the keypad. Still no luck. The other door goes up and down.

Now the smoke in the garage is really billowing. I get back in the driver's seat and notice that my oil gauge is all the way to the right. In desperation, I finally call Lane. "I know you're at work. Just tell me what you think this is."

At first, he tells me not to drive. Then he says, "The smoke isn't from under the hood, just the exhaust pipe? That makes no sense. And your oil indicator is on?"

Suddenly the air clears outside my car. No smoke. The oil indicator moves into the normal range. *Great, I can drive.* I back out, then once again try the remote. Both doors come down and click shut, and I hurriedly drive to work.

*What did I do to you today?* I wonder to Alice, then answer myself out loud. "Is this because I lost something from Shady Hill yesterday?"

I know it is. Alice is upset and rightly so. True, the watch with the white-gold band and diamond is old, a wind-up, and no safety chain; but I love it and think of Aunt Jo every time I wear it. Last

Noel Brock

night when I got home, it wasn't on my arm. Obviously, I'm not the only one who misses it.

After I finally get to work today, I call everywhere I was yesterday but no one has seen the watch. I place an ad in the newspaper: Substantial reward. Make someone happy today. Anything to keep from making those brown eyes blue.

# CHAPTER 45

*The winds will blow,*
*Soon to die away.*
*My fair lady*
*Home may she stay.*

## September 2004

The hurricane season started early this year. Bonnie, Charley, Frances, and Ivan have threatened the east coast of Florida. With each storm, I pray for the safety of relatives, even the safety of my grandparents' old home place at Shady Hill. I don't want to see it damaged. I am also afraid for Alice to lose her other home. The implications of a full-time ghost are scary.

The August and September storms have hurt Frank's fishing trips to the Big Bend area of Florida. Two of my friends at work gave him a balloon to cheer him up, with the message, "Hope you're fishing *reel* soon."

Tonight in my living room I'm working on a project for the hospital when Frank's helium balloon, held down by a weight, starts dancing around the room. *Goodness!* It goes up and down, just like the woman who bought my wicker furniture described about her own haunted house. I'm unnerved, but I know Frank is in the other room so I finish my project.

*Truthfully,* I think to Alice, *if I let you interrupt me every time you decide to intrude on the family, I'd never get anything done.*

Abby and Cathy at work tell me there would be a lot of undone stuff at their houses if Alice went home with them. They do worry a little, since they know she has come as far as the office.

I laugh to Frank, telling him his fish balloon is moving because Alice is as anxious as he is for him to go fishing—because what fun she has with me when he's gone!

Another hurricane, Jeanne, is headed to Florida. I'll be glad when this season is over. Hopefully the house on Riverview Drive will still be standing.

# CHAPTER 46

*A story to share*
*And a happy smile.*
*These are blessings*
*That make life worthwhile.*

## September 23, 2004

A diversity class, a budget meeting, and a lunch interview with an applicant for a technical position. And I thought today would be boring.

Dr. Cusson joins the job applicant and me for lunch. Casey, who is from Arlington, Virginia, expresses her desire to find an old colonial home in Masseyville, if she gets the job that is. She confides that she just loves old antebellum homes. She has previously lived in three old homes and, to her delight, one of them was haunted.

I'm debating whether to acknowledge my expertise of this taboo subject when the handsome Dr. Cusson speaks up. "My parents have a ghost in their home in North Carolina." He glances at me sternly, as one looks at a nonbeliever. "You can believe it or not, but William lives there and thinks he's part of the family."

*Not to worry about me,* I think.

Noel Brock

Then I chime in with my Alice experiences, starting with some stories about Shady Hill. When my lunch friends ask for more, I continue. By the time we leave Bali's Café, we all have given and received much and I've had a great time. I received instant credibility… and realized that was an issue for me.

And yes, Casey was offered the position. In the end, however, she decided to stay in Virginia.

I will always remember the day Dr. Cusson and I shared our secret stories with a stranger and became better friends.

## CHAPTER 47

*One day at a time.*

### September 30, 2004

Jen has agreed to help me recover the fabric seats of the dining-room set—as long as I promise we won't make *anyone* mad. She wants no repeat performance of the mystical manifestations at her house.

"Jen, you did a great job picking out this pattern," I say. The floral mauve, peach, and blue material is perfect for the chairs.

Smiling, she picks up a chair bottom and holds it in the air to measure it. All of a sudden, her diamond bracelet hurls off her arm and flies across the room, *way* across the room, with her arm still stationary in the air. "What the heck? Now, look what we've done."

I retrieve the bracelet from the living-room doorway, and Jen scrutinizes the entire room nervously, visibly upset. "If this were my house, moving would be the first order of the day."

## Noel Brock

I respond defensively. "You make it sound so simple. I can't just up and leave. Remember, 'Whither Thou Goest, I Will Go.'"

Jen rolls her dark eyes, then staples the last chair bottom. "Read my lips. I would M-O-V-E."

# CHAPTER 48

*I have seen spirits where in castles they roam,*
*But never in a home sweet home.*

## October 1, 2004

My friend, Carleigh, knows about ghosts and surreal things like haunted castles. She's from England. She has wanted to visit my house to see if she picks up any "vibes." We settle on this Friday evening while my guys are out of town.

Carleigh has fascinating tales of London: the cathedrals, castles, and the spirits that wander about them. She tells me of the ghost from King Charles II's time who lives in Arundel Castle in Sussex; known as the "Blue Man," he browses books in the library. Evidently, Dover Castle in Kent also has numerous ghosts and a door that creaks where there is no door.

"Sounds familiar," I say.

Frankly, I want to talk about something else, anything else. Carleigh will leave Kennen Road for the night and I will not.

She walks into the living room after dinner and chooses Frank's new recliner. "The pepper steak and asparagus were delicious!" she says. When my phone rings, she says, "Go ahead, I'm fine." I carry my cordless phone into the dining room for privacy.

Fine is not how I find Carleigh when I return to the living room. The television has turned itself on and the ceiling lights turned themselves off. She's sitting in the dark, watching *Law and Order*. "Not by choice," she says.

When we hear a faint whistle from somewhere, with a very proper British accent and a hint of terror she says, "Nothing quite like this in my country. Perhaps there is a better day for me to come back. You don't have to show me out." She starts to the door, leaving her dessert behind, and I run to catch her. "No worry," she says. "I will fetch it another time."

After Carleigh is sitting in her car, she turns to me. "Noel, whatever, you see in this place is beyond me. Give me Pengersick Castle, or Sherborne Castle with Sir Walter Raleigh's ghost, any day of the week." She seems more relaxed now and she laughs. "What fun we had. Have a good evening!"

Carleigh waves goodbye as she drives her Audi out of the circular driveway. I go back inside. It's going to be a long evening, and an even longer night.

# CHAPTER 49

*A hug without a face,*
*Footsteps without a trace.*

## October 4, 2004

I wake up trying to breathe. What a nightmare! Frank is snoring on the other side of our king-sized bed. I struggle to sit up and try to remember my dream. Someone had me in an embrace and was holding me around my waist so tightly that I woke up gasping for air.

It wasn't a dream. I can still feel the arms around me, like a giant bear hug. Shaking, I prop my pillows behind me and lean against them.

Then I hear footsteps in the hallway, moving slowly away from the bedroom. My heart races and for a long time I don't move.

*I don't want to be hugged or touched by a ghost,* I think firmly. But I have been.

Hours later, much-coveted sleep finally comes and the rest of the night is peaceful.

## Noel Brock

But in the morning, I waken with a very sore rib cage. "Frank, you will not believe this when I tell you."

The trouble here is anyone will believe just about anything.

# CHAPTER 50

*Some spots are cold,*
*Some rooms are hot.*
*A research lab*
*This house is not.*

## October 6, 2004

Late one night I'm on the phone with Lindy, a friend, when the doorbell rings. Holding my cordless phone, I peek out the curtains on the door window. After all, it is midnight. Seeing no one, I go to the front door and look out. The door chime is still resonating through the hallway... but no one is at the door.

Then the doorbell ceases to ring and I continue my conversation with Lindy. She has someone she wants me to meet, Ted Mylar, a paranormal psychologist from Dallas. She has told him about Alice and he has some studies he wants to conduct.

"Sorry," I say. "I know you mean well, but things will have to get a lot worse before I have ghost equipment on my living-room floor."

She laughs. "You worry about the *equipment* in your house?"

Lindy tells me this Paranormal Research Company provides

knowledge and research and does intervention if necessary. Supposedly they use meters, cameras, and infrared equipment to see what they're dealing with. They mostly handle worst-case scenarios, and usually consult a priest or a minister to help conquer the phenomena.

"All this sounds way too technical and serious for my problem," I say. "Alice is usually well-behaved, and she causes no major discomfort or extreme fear."

Really I'm nervous about where all this would be going, and do I really want to get rid of Alice?

"Actually," I say to Lindy, "I've already talked to a chaplain, at a business seminar dinner."

It had been comfortable talking to a stranger. He laughed so hard that at first I concluded either he didn't believe me, or believed but didn't know how to help me.

Reverend Terry later confided his own similar story about an aunt who also had a ghost, except that she left her lovely old Maryland home into which she had recently moved. He smiled. "My Aunt Sara doesn't have a sense of humor about such things."

# CHAPTER 51

*Wonder it.*
*You have heard.*
*Believe it.*
*You have seen.*

## October 7, 2004

The crisp autumn day is too perfect to be in a doctor's office, so I sit in a chair by the window to feel the sun coming through. An October copy of the *Masseyville Highlights* has articles of haunted houses in our town. All the homes are antebellum style and most of them are familiar to me. One is the Bell House, now a two-story restaurant. Waiters interviewed described blenders turning on spontaneously, a candle flickering without a flame, a Confederate soldier appearing in the north-wing banquet room. The owner confirmed that he also had seen the soldier and heard slamming doors. I close my eyes and remember my own experience at the Bell House.

It's 1967. Jen and I and several friends are having a fun evening. One of our dare-devil things to do is visit "haunted places."

## Noel Brock

We've heard that an old-abandoned house on University Street has ghostly apparitions. As teenagers do, we excitedly head to the house in Jen's blue Chevrolet Belair. Judy recognizes the once-elegant white house as the old Bell place. Her grandmother used to play there as a child.

Nervously, the five of us go up to the unlocked front door and sneak inside. Nothing happens, so we move into the parlor; then cautiously start up the winding staircase to the second floor. Since Jen and I are the experienced ghost hunters, we lead the way. The two boys and Judy are shaking in anticipation.

Just as we get to the top, our flashlight goes out and one of the bedroom doors slams shut. Our screams echo throughout the empty house. We run down the stairs in pitch black. It isn't easy, but we manage to do it.

Out on the sidewalk all is quiet… too quiet. Paul and I realize the others have jumped into the blue Chevy and left us on the sidewalk. When we see a police cruiser coming, I want to go back inside the house and hide.

"I'd rather go to jail," Paul says, "than back into that house."

The front porch and surrounding bushes protect us until Jen drives up and rescues us. Paul and I climb into our get-a-way car and he gives me a look of incredulity, because I am not scared.

In the car, I tell the group, "Just think, Jen and I get to have these experiences frequently at Shady Hill. You all need to come with us sometime."

"No thanks," they answer in unison.

Back in the present, I laugh and continue reading the article. One patron at the Bell House Restaurant described her horror at seeing a bearded man in a gray uniform moving down the hallway outside the women's restroom. She didn't stop to pay her bill that night.

I smile. *One has to experience it.*

# CHAPTER 52

*Just like a picture*
*Plain as the day,*
*A vision of blue.*
*What can I say?*

## October 8, 2004

"Why do *I* never see Alice?" I ask Abby one morning at work.

Our conversation concerns another strange occurrence at Kennen Road. Always sounds, smells, touches. Some shadows and sporadic misty vapors. Many mechanical maneuvers, too numerous to count. Yet never have *I* seen the lady in blue, although I feel her presence as real as if she is standing next to me.

"Think of the people who have seen Alice," I say. "My grandparents, my mom, Aunt Jo, their friends, all those airmen, all those men at Cape Kennedy, Lauren's husband in Orlando, Leigh, the visitor to the condo at Melbourne Beach, and Lane. They've all seen her. Even Allison saw the blue shadow in the doorway to Lane's room. And remember Miss Mady in our office?"

Abby is pensive. "Well, you and Jen almost saw her at Shady

## The Lady in Blue

Hill when you were children and the blue vapor was materializing into a woman. Maybe she took to heart your reaction at that time. After all, you *are* the hostess now and she is the guest in *your* home. Maybe she's just waiting for the right time."

"I hope when she does come to dinner that Frank will be there and see her, too. His reaction will be worth it!"

We both laugh and Abby wonders out loud if she might see Alice some day.

"As long as you don't tell me she's a passenger in my car," I say. "Remember, I don't do carpools."

Abby grins. "Oh, yeah?"

# CHAPTER 53

*A bride and her bouquet,*
*No matter the century*
*It is done the same way.*

## October 9, 2004

A bright light flashes in the dining room, beside the chair where Lane's tux is hanging over the back. I rush in and look around. As I'm watching, one corner of the tablecloth goes from being folded on the right to being folded on the left. A chill goes through me and I yell to Frank. "There's something in the dining room!" He comes in and just looks at me as if to say, *There's always something in the dining room.*

The next morning, Lane tries on the tuxedo which he will wear tonight to the wedding of a good buddy. Frank and I assure him that the length is right on the slacks and the sleeves of the jacket. I am slightly distracted, though, and staring into space; as usual thinking about Alice. It's October and that's when she first presented herself at our house here in Georgia. It's been six years now and I'm still not sure why she came.

## The Lady in Blue

Then I remember something important. *The wedding that never happened at Shady Hill was to be in October. Could that be the reason she came to us in the fall of 1998?*

I voice my thoughts out loud and Frank says, "This is 2004. That was ninety-nine years ago."

Everyone seems to think I should be used to these strange phenomena by now—but never does one get used to it. At best, I can now acknowledge the bizarre happenings without going into hysteria as in earlier days.

Now there's another October wedding. My mom and dad, Cassie and Ron, are celebrating their fifty-eighth anniversary on October 12. In many ways how much their lives have remained the same. Alice is still here.

# CHAPTER 54

*Can you see what I see?*
*Delicate bluebells in design.*
*Can you hear what I hear?*
*Chiming cymbals so divine.*

## December 2004

Without a doubt Alice resides at least part of the time in Masseyville, Georgia at my house. Where she goes when she's not here, I don't know.

Over the years when visiting relatives near Shady Hill, I have always driven past the old home place. These days the picture-perfect house of yesterday looks neglected. The fuchsia azalea bushes that used to bloom nine months out of the year are gone. The palm tree in front is bent from withstanding many tropical storms. The black shutters are painted blue on the white-framed house. The front porch has stuff stacked up in piles and there are no comfortable gliders or chairs in a row. Still, I have a burning desire to go inside one more time.

Recently I wrote a letter to the owner who purchased the house from the Cason family twenty years ago. I asked her two things:

# The Lady in Blue

permission to visit Mama's house, at her convenience of course; and has she ever encountered Alice?

This morning the phone rings and it's Mrs. Ford inviting me to her house anytime I'm in Shady Hill. It's what else she tells me that is dumbfounding. *She* has a ghost, too.

Mrs. Ford's ghost is fairly vague and appears infrequently. Her dog and cat on occasion cross through the hallway door and stop in mid step, the hair on their backs standing on end. Her daughter-in-law, Margo, won't even stay at the Riverview house alone. Mrs. Ford's voice trembles, and I hope my seeking answers has not ruined her peace and tranquility.

One thing I do wonder, *Does Alice live in her Florida home, too?*

# CHAPTER 55

*In the misty moonlight*
*One hundred years ago,*
*What tragedy that fateful night.*
*Love enables us to know.*

## January 2005

On my next trip to Florida, I persuade Frank to stop at Shady Hill. Mrs. Ford knows I'm coming.

To be back inside Mama and Denny's home after nearly twenty years is exciting, from my viewpoint anyway. Frank isn't thrilled.

Everything is so different. The decor is casual and country; my grandmother had mixed-formal with wicker and rattan. The colors are now dark; Mama loved aqua, mint-green, and white. The windows are closed and covered; Mama always had breezes blowing in. There's no living room or dining room; it's now a great room with a pool table. The mostly glass sunroom on the backside of the house has been closed in for storage, and the brick fireplace is cold and empty. The house has lost its charm and itself looks like a ghost of yesteryears.

A brief step out the back door shows that a lemon tree has re-

## The Lady in Blue

placed the orange tree, and the banana tree is gone. The strong citrus smell is pleasant but not the fragrance to which I romped and played in this yard at the age of four. A lot of potted ferns now decorate the porch.

Back inside the house, standing in the dining-room archway, I remember the cold blast of artic-like air that used to freeze me on a hot summer day… and Mama didn't have air conditioning. Was I only ten when Jen and I saw the blue vapor materializing into a lady in blue? I shiver, thinking it's from the memory. Then I realize I'm feeling *the cold spot.*

Mrs. Ford is cheerfully talking to Frank. I guess she's lonely living here by herself. Then I hear someone else in the house, someone crying softly. Apparently Mrs. Ford and Frank don't hear it. I move closer to the mournful sound.

*Oh, Alice, why do you weep? Is it still 1905 and you are looking for Larry? Or are you weeping for your second family, the Casons? Is it 1944 and Denny has typhus fever, or 1971 and he's dying of cancer? Maybe it's 1982 when Mama Cason takes her last breath, or 1989 when Hugh has survived World War II but succumbs to cancer? Are you crying over Aunt Jo's death in 2001, or Randy's in 2002?*

I wonder why Alice cries for those gone on to the life after death… when all she has to do is follow the light and go with them?

I do not fear this lady in blue. I am sad for her and deeply sorrowed for her suspension somewhere between life and death. I feel like weeping.

I hurry Frank's conversation with Mrs. Ford and move out onto the porch where I watch the moonlight gliding across the river. I am twenty-five again, rocking and chatting with Mama Cason.

"Whoever this ghost is," Mrs. Ford says, "she comes and she goes."

I smile, because I know. Alice spends time with all of her families: occasionally at Shady Hill, looking for her lost lover and former family; and with her new best friends, the Casons.

However, Shady Hill is not Alice's home anymore. She doesn't know this family, and the house and furnishings are not recognizable.

Alice moved in with Aunt Jo in Orlando until she died. Then Alice came to Georgia. No wonder she made such a commotion when I sent the dining-room set to be refinished. No wonder the picture of my grandmother's house *cried*. There is so little left to link this lady in blue to her life at Riverview Drive, she doesn't want to lose the few ties she has left.

"You know," Mrs. Ford says, "the family who built this house in the late 1880s sent to Georgia for the wood to construct it."

*Sent to Georgia? Maybe Alice's family has ties to Georgia as well?*

Mrs. Ford promises to send me a copy of the historical abstract of the house if she can find it. I look at the many boxes of papers beside her desk and figure I'll never get that coveted information.

Frank and I thank Mrs. Ford and leave. As we pull out the long sandy driveway at 8311 Riverview Drive, I look back. Then I look in the empty backseat of our car.

"Just checking," I say to Frank and smile.

ISBN 1412069955-5